Karen M

As a teenager growing up in Aberdeen, Scotland, Karen McCombie had three clear objectives:

work as a graphic artist;

never leave Scotland;

never get married.

But fate has a funny way of messing with things and Karen is now a full-time writer, living in leafy North London with her husband and an interesting collection of cats.

Prior to this she worked as a journalist on a variety of magazines, including *J17* and *Sugar*, and began her book-writing career with several teen novels published under pseudynoms – including many for the *Sugar Secrets...* range.

Under her own name, Karen is author of the bestselling *Ally's World* series, as well as several more teen novels.

When she's not writing, Karen's top five hobbies are watching videos (preferably with a takeaway curry), going to gigs, reading, patting cats and belly-dancing. You can find out more about Karen on her website:

www.karenmccombie.com

In sarah's shadow

Karen McCombie

HarperCollins *Children's Books*

For the four girls at Greylshe Girls' School
who helped inspire a plot twist. (You know who you are!)

First published in Great Britain by CollinsFlamingo 2003
CollinsFlamingo is an imprint of HarperCollins*Publishers* Ltd,
77-85 Fulham Palace Road, Hammersmith,
London W6 8JB

The HarperCollins *Children's Books* website address is:
www.harpercollinschildrensbooks.co.uk

2

Text © Karen McCombie 2003

ISBN 0 00 712680 8

Karen McCombie asserts the moral right to
be identified as the author of the work.

Printed and bound in England by
Clays Ltd, St Ives plc

PART ONE
Out from the shadows

Megan's story

Chapter 1

Charmed, I'm sure...

There's always a flip side to everything, isn't there?

For every good bit of news, there's bad. For every amazing piece of luck, there's a dog poo waiting to be stepped in. For every silver lining, there's a big, fat cloud. For everyone who's charmed, someone's jinxed. For every Sarah, there's a Megan...

"Hey, Sweetpea, what's with you?" Dad beams as Sarah bounces through the living room doorway. "You look pleased with yourself!"

Ah, yes... and for every Sweetpea, there's a Pumpkin. 'Cause in our family, my sister Sarah is the bringer of good news; the one who has amazing luck; the girl with her own in-built silver lining; the charmed eldest child with the pretty pet name to go with her pretty self.

Then there's Megan (ie, me): the bringer of bad news; the one destined to tread in the dog poo; the girl lurking under the big, fat cloud; the jinxed younger sister with the pet name as round and lumpen as—

"Put your legs down, Pumpkin!" Mum orders me, practically shooing me off the sofa I've been curled up on since I got home from school. "Let your sister sit down!"

All praise Princess Sarah! She hath arrived and we must all bow low to Her Loveliness. Wonder if I should wipe away any grime left behind from my trainers before she graces the sofa with her wondrous bottom?

Nah. I won't bother.

Oh, God – I know how bad that sounds. I'm coming over like a total bitch, aren't I? But I'm not... *honest* I'm not. Just ask anyone who feels like they're the least loved kid when it comes to their parents and they'll know exactly what I'm going through. After fourteen years of watching my parents and Sarah indulge in this mutual appreciation society, it's like I'm this invisible member of my own family, somehow surplus to requirements. Think of it that way and you'll see it's hard not to sound bitter and twisted sometimes, but all I really am is hurt, hurt, *hurt*.

Specially when I spot those snidey, sideways looks

Sarah sometimes throws my way when she thinks I don't notice...

"Come on then, Sarah! What's put that smile on your face?" says Dad excitedly, setting aside his newspaper and giving his favourite child his full attention. Mum's the same, turning the sound down on the local news she's been watching on TV and gazing at my sister expectantly.

Sarah shrugs her fluffy-collared coat off her shoulders and shakes free her sheeny-shiny chestnut hair. Where does she think she is? At an audition for a shampoo ad? The steps outside the Met Bar, with the whirr of cameras and catcalls of the paparazzi all around? Doesn't she realise that this is just our normal front room, with its normal floral wallpaper border and a normal family sitting around on our extremely normal sofa and chairs? Ah, but maybe *that's* it; maybe that hair-tossing business is for *my* benefit. You know, just to remind me that my dull, brown fuzz of a hairdo can never compete with hers.

Oh yeah, Sarah likes to let me know my place, but it's in these subtle, paper-cut sharp ways that can only be seen by the trained eye. And believe me, I'm trained. After a lifetime of being related to Princess Perfect sitting here next to me, you get wise.

Sarah is just about to speak, when Mum starts fluttering and clucking around her as usual.

"Oh, don't crush your new coat, darling!" she frowns in concern, indicating Sarah's long, fawn, sheepskin coat. "Pumpkin – go and hang it up for your sister!"

I'm about to say something – like, why doesn't Sarah hang up her own coat? – but there's no point. Instead of Mum realising how unfair that is, she'll just think I'm being unhelpful and grumpy, instead of bright and smiley, like you-know-who. So instead, I put my magazine down on the floor, wordlessly hold my hand out and wait for Sarah to pass me her stupid coat, like I'm her handmaiden or something.

"Stop fussing, Angela!" I hear Dad jovially tell my mum off as I head out into the hall. "Let the girl talk!"

What a joke, eh? Dad tells Mum off for the heinous crime of stalling Sarah's latest piece of good news, in her never-ending stream of amazing luck. He doesn't nark at Mum for ordering me about; it's as if I came as a package deal with the house ('1930s semi with garage; servant included').

"Well…" Sarah begins from the comfort of the sofa, but I'm outside in the hall now, burying my face into the soft-as-clouds furry collar of this amazing sheepskin coat. Not that I want it – if *I* wore it, I'd look like… well, a *sheep*. Whereas Sarah – with her matching boots, knee-length denim skirt and tight black top – looks like she just stepped out of the pages of a style magazine.

If only I was taller, slimmer, less round in places I shouldn't be and more round in places I should; maybe then I'd have people staring at me in the street like Sarah does; maybe then I'd be less invisible.

And then I smell it – the cloying, sickly-sweet scent that Sarah always smothers herself in. It jars in my head and sends a sharp pain shooting through my sinuses. I quickly pull my face away from it and chuck the coat towards the row of hooks on the wall, but I miss and it crumples into a pale heap on the floor. I grab it up roughly, then chuck it towards the rack again, not bothering to search among the white fluffy fibres for a clothes hoop for hanging. Instead, the coat dangles lopsidedly, swaying gently, an ugly bulge already pressing through the suede where the hook juts out.

There'll be a mark if I leave it like that... I think guiltily. Automatically, I reach over to hang it properly, then hear Sarah's boastful words waft out of the living room, as if she's deliberately raised her voice so I don't miss what she's got to say.

"...and that's when Mr Fisher said – 'I want you, Sarah!'"

I want you, Sarah... to shut up, for once? I say to myself, feeling the blood pound in my veins.

I want you, Sarah... to leave the country and never come back?

I want you, Sarah... to have, just for once, the tiniest bit of bad luck – just enough so you know what life feels like for the mere mortals who have to live in your shadow?

All of a sudden, I snatch my hand from Sarah's crumpled coat, turning away from it and the ugly bulge, and walk back into the living room. It's petty and pathetic, I know, but you can't begrudge a girl a bit of petty and pathetic revenge now and then, specially in the face of a sister who gets the strangest kick out of making her feel useless...

Somehow, I don't feel like sitting back down next to her – maybe Sarah's silver lining is radiating too much ultra-violet light for a thin-skinned person like me to stand. Instead, I perch on the arm of Mum's chair and try and figure out what exactly Sarah's boasting on about this time.

"So, Mr Fisher chose you, out of *how* many people, Sarah?" Mum asks, practically prickling with static electricity she's so proud.

"Well, there were about thirty people at the auditions today, and I think he saw more people yesterday," Sarah smiles a golden-child smile. "But today he finally decided on which five to pick for the band line-up."

"And when is the actual Battle of the Bands competition happening?"

That's Dad, perched now on the edge of his seat. He couldn't look more excited if he suddenly saw his Lotto numbers sliding next to each other on the TV screen.

I get it. This Battle of the Bands thing – there are posters all over the noticeboards at school about it. It's this regional competition that's on at the end of next month – all the schools in the area enter a band, and the winners get a free pair of drumsticks from the competition sponsors or whatever. It's pretty good fun; I was in the audience for it last year and there were some really brilliant bands there, and some spectacularly naff ones too, but it was a great afternoon's skive. I hadn't realised Sarah was going in for it this time around. I mean, I know she can sing (well, she can do anything, can't she?) and she's taught herself to play guitar this year (in between getting top grades in her exams, having an amazing social life and being all-round fantastic). But then she wouldn't tell me, would she? She's not even bothering to look at me now; she's saving all her smiles for her appreciative audience of two.

"Who else is in the band with you? Did Cherish and Angel get picked?" asks Mum.

I realise I'm scratching at my wrists and stop. It's a nervous habit and I don't mean to do it, but it just happens. It really winds Mum up.

"Yes, they got picked too. And there's this guy Conor who's going to play bass and a lad called Salman who's going to be on drums. I *kind* of know both of them, but just to say hi to."

I rack my brains. Cherish and Angel – of *course* I know them, since they've been best friends with Sarah for years, regularly swanning in and out of our house (and blanking me, usually). But Salman and Conor... well, I'm pretty sure there's a Salman in the Upper Sixth, but I don't know about a Conor – there're loads of Conors at our school.

"And so what happens now?"

That's Dad again, probably already envisaging some glittering musical career for Sarah. Sorry, Daddy dearest; don't suppose she'll be opening for U2 any time soon. Then again, knowing *her* luck...

"Well," Sarah says brightly, "we'll have to get together with Mr Fisher and work out what song we want to play, then it'll be a case of loads of rehearsals up until the competition!"

They'll probably win. I haven't heard them play together and I haven't seen the two blokes, but unless they make a real mess of it or the guys look like extras out of *Planet of the Apes*, then it's in the bag. How could the judges pass over a band that's got the three prettiest, coolest girls in our school in it?

Oh, boy... Sarah's swollen head is just about to get that *bit* more hot-air balloon-sized. Winning the competition will be a case of yet *more* glory landing slap-bang in her lap, just like it always does. Unlike me, who can't scrape past average in any given exam. The only competitions I ever bother to enter are for give-aways in magazines. And guess what? 'Free glitter make-up!! 1000s of sets up for grabs!!! To everyone except Megan Collins!' I'll tell you what my luck's like: if I buy a magazine with a free gift on the cover, I won't notice the gift's been nicked off it till I'm outside the shop and can't complain. And round about then is the time I'll step in the dog poo and get soaked by an unexpected black cloud's worth of rain.

God, I'm off on one again, aren't I? I'm sorry. It's just hard when you don't feel like one of life's shiny, happy people. And it's even harder when one of life's shiny, happy people lives in the room across the hall from you.

"Megan, don't do that!"

Mum's voice is soft and urgent, her cool fingers are pressing mine still. I hadn't realised I'd been scratch-scratching at my wrists again. And now they're all looking at me. Looking at the freak member of their family with the scars on my skin that remind me and them of just how imperfect I am.

"I've got homework," I mumble and get out of the room, away from the pitying, uncomfortable glances that are focused on me. They're better off without me around, spoiling my parents' fun as they soak up the sparkles of Sarah's success.

"Megan...!"

I hope Mum doesn't follow me – I don't want her to. I hate those cosy pep talks she tries to give me, when she perches on the edge of my bed and always ends up upset, holding my hands and turning them over so she can stroke the jagged, bumpy white marks running longways across the raised tendons and blood vessels. And then she starts crying, like she always does, as if every time she touches them it's as shocking as that first time when she found me...

I'll stick on my headphones; that's what I'll do. Listen to something loud, so loud that there's no room in my head for Sarah and her ten trillion lucky breaks.

My hand wraps around cool metal and I'm about to

close the door of my room, to shut the whole world out, when I glance across the hallway into Sarah's room. There's her guitar, propped up against the desk, a reminder of how much Fate likes to smile down on my sister while leaving me stuck in the shadows.

Any chance *I* can get a turn in the luck department? Please? Maybe sometime this century?

Chapter 2

Wonderful things happen... to other people

"It looks nice!"

Pamela, my best friend, is lying. It's something she does pretty regularly.

"It *doesn't* look nice," I tell her as I stare at my bizarre reflection in the full-length hall mirror. "It looks crap. Before, I had *no* boobs, and now – now it looks like I've got two satsumas shoved up my T-shirt."

"But in a *good* way!" Pamela shrugs uselessly. "Maybe you just need to slacken the straps or something... so they're not so high."

High, as in tucked just below my chin, where – unless I'm very much mistaken – boobs aren't meant to be. Well, bang goes two weeks' allowance on a Wonderbra that probably does wonderful things for other girls but makes me look like a *freak*.

"You've really got to be more positive, Pumpkin!" Mum had told me this morning when she caught me hugging a cushion across my non-existent chest while sighing at the sight of Destiny's Child bouncing around in spangly bras that could barely contain their bosoms on some old video they were rerunning on MTV.

"Be more positive": that's what Mum always tries to tell me if I'm down about anything. Maybe if she stopped calling me Pumpkin for five minutes I might feel more positive, of course. (Just a thought.) But you know, like most human beings, mothers can't be wrong *all* the time, so I decided to try and do the positive thing, just this once, just to keep her happy. And so this afternoon (spent shopping and window-shopping, like every other Saturday), me and Pamela wandered into the underwear department at BhS, laughed at all the old lady knickers (big enough to hold a week's worth of groceries, if you sewed the legs up), sniggered at the G-strings (not enough pant to cover a postage stamp, never mind your girly bits), and bought myself a slinky, black Wonderbra. Which I am now wearing, and which is making me feel about as slinky as a baboon in a fairground hall of mirrors.

"Hold on…" says Pamela, and before I can stop her she's got her hands up the back of my top and is trying to wrestle the straps a little looser. "There! Now if I just do *this*… how's that? Better, huh?"

Better… no, I don't think so.

In front of me, all I can see is a girl wearing size 12-14 black trousers, a boy's (aged twelve) grey Gap T-shirt, with two satsumas loitering in the middle of her chest (one higher than the other), while a hand holds up her dull, brown hair in what is supposed to look like a loose and lovely topknot but is more like a gently collapsing bird's nest.

God, I'd be irresistible, if I wasn't such a walking disaster…

"You might as well let it go," I tell Pamela, wriggling away from her hand and feeling my hair tumbling down over my shoulders. "It still looks lousy, whatever you try to do to it."

Maybe I should grow my hair really long – that way I could drape it over my chest so no one would see that I don't actually *have* one.

"Just trying to help," Pamela mumbles, taking a step away from me.

I *know* she's trying to help; she always does. But sometimes, the more Pamela tries to help, the more she puts her foot in it. Like the time she convinced me that the silver, spray-on hair glitter I bought looked excellent? I wasn't so sure, but decided to believe her and wore it to the end-of-term Christmas party. Lucky it *was* the end of term; the nickname of "Granny" that the boys dumped on me that night – on account of my new-look 'grey' hair – had been forgotten by the time the next term started, thank God. Even if *I* still remembered.

"Look, you want a coffee?" I ask her, realising that Pamela's acting like I've slapped her in the face.

"OK," she replies, following me, lap-dog style, through to the kitchen.

Poor Pamela; she has to put up with me and my stupid black moods, but it's cool – she knows how hard things get for me. It's not as if Pamela's life is some rose-tinted success story – me and her are neck-and-neck when it comes to being resoundingly average at school – but at least her size 12 body is all in proportion, even if she isn't exactly Kate Moss gorgeous, and at least she doesn't have an older sister who's so stunning in every department that she can't help but feel like the family booby prize by comparison.

Course, there is one area where my best friend is scoring considerably better than me.

"You said you'd show me the message Tariq texted

you," I nod in the direction of the bag Pamela left on the kitchen stool when she came round to collect me earlier.

I know what the message says, of course: Pamela only told me about twelve thousand times this afternoon. But then she's desperate to dig out her mobile and show me the message for real, and if that gets her smiling again then I'll act surprised (as surprised as she was to get a message like that) when she sticks it under my nose.

"Look, see?" she beams as, right on cue, the jumble of text letters dance in front of my eyes, just as I flip the kettle on.

"*Hi, Pammie – what's up? Tar x,*" I read aloud, my voice practically drowned out by Pamela hyperventilating.

Not the most romantic message in the world; not exactly an excerpt from the love scenes between Joey and Dawson in *Dawson's Creek*. But it's enough to make Pamela feel like the most desired female in the Western hemisphere and I have to say I'm a tiny bit jealous, even though Tariq is the sort of boy I'd have to kiss with a paper bag on my head if we were ever in that last boy/last girl on Earth scenario.

"See? I told you! 'X' is a kiss, isn't it?" Pamela babbles, stabbing at the phone and nearly erasing her precious message.

"'Course it's a kiss!" I grin, idly wondering if 'x' stands for kiss in all languages. What if 'x' is short-hand for 'sod off' in Vietnamese? But luckily for Pamela, Tariq is from north London, same as us, and so 'x' is most definitely a kiss and most definitely unexpected, since the only communication Pamela and Tariq have had so far is a few shy "hi"s across a crowded dinner hall. Who did he get her number from? What gave him the courage to call? And why's he suddenly calling her "Pammie" when no-one else in the world ever has?

"*Pammie...*" says Pamela wistfully, leaning up against the gently gurgling fridge.

I guess it sounds more exotic than plain Pamela (in the same way chocolate digestives are more exotic than plain ones). Pamela Ann Jones: not the most memorable name in the world, as Pamela would be the first to agree. Not even an 'e' on the end of Ann for that extra scrap of glamour. But don't get me wrong; I'm not putting her down for having a dullish name; after all, mine is only just a fraction more interesting. It's just that it's ironic, isn't it, that my best friend happens to be called Pamela, while Sarah's two best mates are named Cherish and Angel. Cherish Kofi and Angeline Girardot, to be precise. Memorable by name, memorable in the flesh, as most of the boys at Bakerfield School will happily tell you, if only they can get their tongues back in their mouths and their jaws off the floor. They're like that about Sarah too (naturally), but I don't want to sully my mind with thoughts of *her* right now. It's been two solid weeks of Sarah, the competition and general parent hysteria *about* Sarah and the competition in this household and, right now, I'm kind of enjoying having the place to myself for five Sarah-free, parent-free minutes...

"So, what are you going to text back to him?" I ask 'Pammie', handing her a mug of milky coffee.

"God! I hadn't thought about that!" Pamela suddenly switches from happiness to panic in half a split second.

Lateral thinking: that's when your mind spins off at different tangents from one particular thought. Pamela, bless her, doesn't do lateral; her mind works in one direction at a time, with blinkers fixed to either side of her brain to stop her from being distracted by incidental stuff. Now I feel bad for her, the last thing I want is to spoil her happiness by making her tense up about a suitable reply.

"How about... *Hi Tar – hanging with Megan. What's up with U? Pammie x,*" I suggest.

"That's brilliant!" Pamela beams. "But could *you* key it in, Megan? My hands are shaking too much..."

"Sure," I shrug, taking the mobile from her and doing my good deed by tapping out the message.

"Hey, that's not right," says Pamela, being a back-seat texter and pointing out the mistake I've just caught myself making.

"Hi Tar – hanging with Sarah—"

My stupid brain has just subconsciously sent traitorous messages through my nervous system, all because I've just heard the front door open and my sister's laughing voice drift down the hall towards us.

"Oh," says Sarah, stopping dead in the kitchen doorway. She's got her wine-coloured velvet jacket on today, with those hipster Levi's of hers that have worn in all the right places.

"Oh?" I shrug back at her, hoping I sound edgier than I feel as I quickly slam down Pamela's phone and fold my arms across my lopsided, satsuma-look boobs. (Wish I'd got Pamela to even up the straps at least...)

Maybe it's worked, me staking my finders-keepers' claim to the kitchen and my right to a private conversation with my friend. Sarah's looking weird: kind of flushed and surprised or something.

And then I see why... and it's nothing to do with me trying (and probably failing) to be edgy or tough with her.

"Conor..." says Sarah, with her voice wavering and

her hands fluttering, "this is my sister Megan. And that's her friend Pamela."

Behind her in the doorway is this tall guy I vaguely recognise from the Upper Sixth, in a denim jacket, with shaggy, fawn-coloured hair flopping around his face and a guitar case – the flash guitar Sarah's borrowed from the music department – slung across one shoulder.

Instantly, I know that something is going on between the two of them. Sarah wouldn't flush pink and act so flustered if it was just one of the regular boy mates she sometimes hangs around with. And regular boy mates don't act the gallant hero and offer to carry your guitar home from rehearsal.

And just as instantly, when Conor's face cracks into a heart-melting smile in my direction, I know that the world is not a fair place.

How else can you explain it when you've just set eyes on your soulmate... and realise he'll never in a million years see *you* the same way?

Chapter 3

Good deeds ⇌ good luck?

"Oh."

That 'oh' doesn't sound too good. The cards on the table – some face down and some weirdly illustrated and facing up, spread out in some strange cross pattern – tell me precisely nothing. But for the old woman sitting across from me, it's like she's deciphering some ancient language or something.

Or maybe she's just making it all up as she goes along.

"I see conflict with someone," she mutters, shaking her head as she talks, sending minuscule whorls of peachy powder drifting from her face into still air that smells dusty, musty and Mr Sheen clean at the same time. "A girl. Someone close... close to you, *and* close in age. Does that make sense to you?"

Two years.

That's all that separates me and Sarah, but it might as well be two decades or two continents for all we have in common. It's been like that as far back as I have memories. Actually, my very first memory – when I was around two, which makes Sarah around four – is of being hot and uncomfortable, wriggling around in Mum's arms in too many layers of knitted clothes and being told off. Why? Because I was distracting her and Dad from watching Sarah doing her one-girl singing sensation show – belting out Kylie Minogue's *I Should Be So Lucky*. Ever since then it seems like I've had years of being told to shush and be quiet while Sarah has sung, skipped, tap-danced and dazzled her way through life.

Me? I'm a trudger – trudging through shifting sands while Sarah jogs right past me on the pavement towards some bright, shining future, which now includes great boyfriends, if Conor is anything to go by...

"It links in here, with this card that points to a feeling of unrest," says the old lady, tapping a ridged, yellowish nail on the illustration of a stooped figure.

"Almost of being weighted down."

I'm finding it hard to concentrate – now that I've let a thought of Conor into my head I know I won't be able to shake his face from my mind for hours. I wish I could stop thinking about him. I wish I could stop my hand from doodling his name every time I've come into contact with pen and paper over the last week. I even caught myself spelling 'Conor' with the alphabet magnets on our fridge door – I only just managed to scramble it (and the 'Sarah sucks' thing I'd spelt out a couple of minutes before) when Dad walked in on me.

"This conflict... there seems to be more to it than meets the eye. Am I right?"

Mrs Harrison tears her gaze from the cards and shoots me a look, which is kind of disconcerting. Well, the heavy blue eyeshadow is what's really disconcerting. That and the peachy layer of powder covering her downy face, like some fuzzy mask. And the coral lipstick. You can't miss the coral lipstick. Where can you buy make-up like that? Is there some secret, old lady make-up counter at the back of big department stores or something? The freaky make-up – that's what's made me (and every other kid in the street) avoid Mrs Harrison like the plague when I was growing up. The batty old mad woman at the house on the corner: she was practically guaranteed to get everyone under the age of twelve's imagination going. If she was that freaky to look at, what must the inside of her house be like? Full of slugs and snails and puppy dogs' tails?

Well, I'm here in Mrs Harrison's house – a double first, since it's also the first time in my life I've ever given her more that a vague, grunted "hello" as I scurried past her garden gate – and it's a disappointment to my over-imaginative, eight-year-old self to see that it looks pretty ordinary. Like most old ladies the world over (my gran and my great grandma included) there's a place for everything and everything in its place. Apart, of course, for the bookshelf that toppled over when she was dusting – the reason she called out to the first person passing (me) to help her lift it up.

Shyness – make that wariness – made me say very little as I followed her inside and lifted the lightweight, flat-pack shelves back upright. Once the job was done, and I'd been in her house just long enough to be surprised by its ordinariness, I thought Mrs Harrison might let me go with a simple thank you, or try and press a Werther's Original (or whatever other strange sweet old people like) into my hand.

Wrong.

And wrong about the ordinary stuff too. "Would you like me to do a tarot reading for you, as my way of saying thanks? I know you young girls love anything to do with horoscopes and seeing into the future."

What I don't like is clichés — that girls my age should be into certain bands or certain TV shows or think certain ways, as if millions and millions of us can be lumped together as one dumb, trivia-obsessed bundle of raging hormones. But in this case, I had to admit Mrs Harrison had a point. Yeah, so maybe I'm the same as so many other people and not as individual as I want to be, but yes, I definitely wanted to see what the future had in store for me. Just as long as please, please, *please* don't let it be more of the same...

This conflict... there seems to be more to it than meets the eye. Am I right? I ran what she'd just said through my head again.

"It's my sister. We don't get along," I shrug, finally giving in and helping Mrs Harrison out with a confirmation or two. "My parents think I'm just jealous of her, but that's not how it is. Not really."

"I see," says Mrs Harrison, glancing from me to the cards that are already face up, and back again.

Does she *really* see? Can those mass-produced, *Lord of the Rings*-style cards really let her peer into my mind, into my life? Can she tell how hard it is to be around someone who constantly puts you down in the smallest, subtlest, almost-invisible-to-the-human-eye way? A self-satisfied smirk in my direction here, a patronising dig there. A few of those a day add up to a lot of dents to a girl's self-esteem over the course of weeks, months, years. Maybe that's what Mrs Harrison is looking at now; not the ordinary, plain me on the outside, but the dented, bruised me on the inside.

Then again, the way her eyes are darting up and down from my face to the cards spread on the table, she might have spotted my scars. Quickly, I pull the sleeves of my fleece down and clutch them tightly in my fists.

An uncomfortable silence suddenly hangs in the air between us, which I realise is her waiting for me to say more about Sarah. But I won't – if she really *can* do this stuff, if she *really* has some kind of a gift, then she doesn't need me to tell her a thing. And if she's just some batty old fake, then I'm not going to give her any more clues that she can use to make up some fantasy future for me.

"Let's take a look at these…" I hear Mrs Harrison

say softly as her strong-looking but wrinkled fingers flip over the last three cards that remain unturned.

The figures on them: they might as well be of Homer, Bart and Lisa Simpson, for all they mean to me. But not to Mrs Harrison, who makes the sort of small, appreciative "ooh" noise that my Mum does when Sarah does a turn in the living room, modelling her latest amazing outfit. Only this "ooh" is all for *me*...

"I see change, lots of change. One phase of your life is ending and a new one is beginning. And with it being in conjunction with these other two cards..."

She pauses, starting up with that tap-tap-tapping of her nail on the laminated illustrations again (but not drumming nearly as fast as my heart is now beating).

"...it's a change that's going to make you very happy. And it's coming soon – sooner than you think."

Change? Happiness? Coming my way soon? My heart is soaring so high I could kiss the thoughtful frown off Mrs Harrison's forehead – only I won't, since I don't want to ruin a beautiful moment by getting peach powder in my mouth...

I've been holding my breath, looking for early sightings of this earth-shattering change coming my way. But life has been depressingly normal: Pamela's been bleating on about her non-blossoming romance with Tariq; every teacher has ignored the fact that there are other subjects – and other teachers – at school and has saddled me with mountains of homework; and Sarah swanned out last night on yet another date with Conor.

I know this last fact because it was me who opened the door to him and had my second ever encounter with that smile. I tell you, no other boy has ever looked at me that intently or smiled at me so warmly in my life. Of course, it only lasted a nanosecond, before Sarah swooped on us, gathering up her coat and Conor, and practically hurtling the poor guy down our garden path.

But I don't care; one nanosecond of that smile will keep me going till next time, whenever that might be. My head's got a snapshot of his face and those friendly, soul-searching brown eyes, firmly fixed, deep in my psyche. And there's a soundtrack on loop too... "Hi, Megan! Hi, Megan! Hi, Megan!" (I've erased the part that said "Is Sarah in?")

"That one's seventy-five pence, love." A voice jars me out of my thoughts.

I glance at the tatty copy of *Catcher in the Rye* I've been holding and quickly put it down.

"No thanks," I shake my head at the pushy guy behind the makeshift table covered in paperbacks.

I'm on my way home from another Saturday hanging out in town with Pamela. This stall: it's parked up outside our local supermarket every weekend afternoon and I've never usually given it a second glance. But a few minutes ago, I found myself hovering, scanning the rows of bright covers, thinking that maybe I should lose myself in a book, to help pass the time till this amazing change decided to make itself known.

But I guess I shouldn't be too impatient. It was only yesterday teatime that Mrs Fruitcake Harrison did her tarot thing on me.

"Go on… I'll make it fifty pence for you!" says the stall guy, forcing *Catcher in the Rye* under my nose again. "It's a classic! It'll be good for your schoolwork!"

Which is exactly why I don't want it. And probably the reason why I'd absent-mindedly picked it up in the first place – we'd read it already in English.

I'm smiling and shaking my head, already stepping away from the book and the hard sell, when something catches my eye. *Witch Way Now?* says a cartoony, gothic, black title on a blood-red book. *Spells To Make Your Life Special!* it says in smaller letters underneath. I can tell from the mock-serious lettering and the exclamation mark that this isn't exactly some ancient tome of historical importance – it's more like a tongue-in-cheek 'spook' cash-in on the back of the Harry Potter phenomenon.

But, cynical or not, I find myself picking it up and flicking through the pages. 'The It Should Have Been Me! Love Spell' makes me smile. I could sure do with some of that. 'The How To Make Him Know I Exist Spell' makes the smile start to fade as I become more intrigued. And then I spot it...

'The Change Your Life Spell'.

"Fancy that one? Won't get you many gold stars from your teachers, a book like that!" I hear the pushy guy guffaw. "Fifty pence for that one, love. As long as you promise to come back and turn it into a fifty quid note once you've got the hang of the spells!"

He thinks he's a real hoot, this bloke. He's not going to get a laugh out of me with pathetic witticisms like that – all he *is* going to get is fifty pence, in the smallest, most annoying pile of change I can rake from the bottom of my purse.

"Oi! You going to be the next Sabrina then!" I hear him call out to me when I'm already halfway down the street.

Of course I'm not the next Sabrina. Of course I don't really believe in magic. But what I do believe in are signs and gut feelings – and maybe (just maybe) this book is the start of it all happening.

Maybe that's rubbish, but so what – it only cost me a bunch of loose coins that were weighing down my bag anyway. And if I'm *right,* well, it could be the best fifty pence I've ever spent...

Chapter 4

Ice and fire...

I feel ridiculous.

According to the book, I need: a beeswax candle (is there any other kind?); a fresh sprig of lavender; an object sacred to me; and a peaceful, quiet room. The trouble is, I don't have any of those. What I *do* have is a cinnamon-scented room freshener candle (unused, unloved Christmas present); some lavender aromatherapy oil (ditto); a copy of PJ Harvey's *Songs from the City, Songs from the Sea* (my favourite rock staress, my all-time favourite CD and therefore my sacred object); and a room that is anything but peaceful, thanks to my dad roaring at the Manchester United versus Someone-or-other football match on the telly downstairs and Sarah twanging away on her guitar in her room across the hall.

"Come on… just do it," I whisper to myself, trying to block out the noise and my feelings of total silliness. The point is, I don't believe in magic, but I *do* believe in doing something symbolic, so if I go through the motions of this – with my reject Christmas presents and *Songs from the City* blaring on my CD player to drown out Manchester United and Sarah's twanging – then I'm being positive. I'm saying if change is going to happen then I'm ready and waiting, not sulking in the corner while good stuff passes me by… (Wow – what would Mum make of that, if she could hear what I'm telling myself?)

First, light the candle…

Great – what with? I don't want to spoil the moment and go trekking downstairs searching for matches. I'll only get the third degree from Mum, hassling me about what exactly I want them for (to light the bonfire under the witch I've got stashed in my bedroom, *obviously*), so instead I just place the candle exactly in front of me on the carpet and stare at it intently, like I'm meditating or something. And then I realise that's pretty stupid, because I need to look away at the book for my next set of instructions.

Move the sprig of lavender above the candle flame in anti-clockwise circles: not close enough to burn it, but enough to let the smell of the lavender infuse the room with its cleansing scent.

OK, so all I have is a small, brown bottle. I twist the cap off and it seems to make more sense to waft it (in anti-clockwise circles, of course) under my nose, so I can actually smell the damn stuff.

Next, hold your sacred object to your heart...

Easy peasy: I grab the empty CD box, with its cover of PJ Harvey striding through a night-time, light-strewn Times Square in New York, and clutch it to my chest. In the background, PJ growls above the roar of guitars.

Now, recite the thing you most want to change in your life.

Wow. How do I choose? Ever since I got the book home and studied this particular spell at close range, it's all I've been able to think about. All through tea tonight, all through Mum and Dad twittering on to Sarah about her day's rehearsal, I just drifted away, trying to figure out my options. And out of a long list of changeable situations (stuff like teachers realising I'm a shy genius rather than an underachieving loser), I settled on the main contenders, which just happened to be...

1. Boobs. Boobs would be good. Two of those – matching, please.
2. Sarah vanishing into thin air – that'd be nice.
3. My parents noticing I exist would be quite a novelty.
4. Conor. Just… Conor.

So how can I choose just one out of all of those? I stare hard at the cinnamon candle, the scent of which – even unlit – mingles headily with the lavender I'm wafting, hug hard on my CD, and whisper…

"Can you *please* let me in there?"

See? This is what it's like. I've only been in the bath five minutes – a bath I announced to everyone that I was having, so no one could complain about no warning and full bladders – and now here's Sarah, banging on the door with yet another loud, bleating demand for me to get out, to make way for her Royal Highness to get in here and floss her Royal Teeth, or whatever, before she goes out for the night. It's not enough for her to rub my nose in it about the great Saturday night she's got planned (some amazing party, I bet, in someone's amazingly huge house in the west end, with the amazingly beautiful Conor to keep her company). Oh no,

41

it doesn't matter that the only thing I've got planned for tonight is a long, lazy bath, with Jim Carrey – courtesy of a DVD – for afters. Sarah *has* to edge her way into my privacy just that *little* bit more, making out like I'm selfish or obstructive or something, lying here among the steamy bubbles. It's got to be for Conor's benefit; Dad's still roaring at the never-ending football match and I can hear Mum cackling away with Auntie Kelly on the phone.

Conor is in Sarah's room right now... when I first ran the bath, I heard them chatting as she let him in the front door and led him up to her room. After that, I turned the taps off and had a deliberately shallow bath, just so I could listen through the walls as Conor began to sing along to the track Sarah was strumming on the guitar.

But now, shallow bath or not, I have to get out of it. I can't relax with her hammering on the door every ten seconds.

"OK, so you've got your way! Satisfied?" I blink at her, hauling open the door and shivering as the chilly January air seeps in through the gaps around the front door and slithers up the stairs to slap my bare, wet skin. Against that, no amount of towelling fabric can keep you warm.

"Yeah, yeah! I just need in for two minutes!" Sarah

glares at me, all pretence of niceness gone – as usual – when Mum and Dad aren't around.

Yeah, yeah. Two minutes, two hours… it doesn't make much difference. Sarah's point was to get me out, to ruin my moment, and she's done it. She wins again, *as* usual.

The bathroom door slams shut behind me and I find myself shivering miserably on the spot, too cold and dejected to move, suddenly too weary of waiting for my 'life change' to do anything but stare off into space, zombie-ing out to the background soundtrack of Dad and the telly roaring, Mum yackety-yacking, and… and… a soft, comforting voice.

"Megan? Are you OK?"

In my frozen moment, I turn my head (a mistake – rapidly cooling beads of water trickle uncomfortably from my wet hair to my goose-pimpling back).

But my bones warm up to centre-of-the-Earth temperatures when I see Conor, perched on the edge of Sarah's bed, arms resting on his knees, those soulful brown eyes staring right at me, reducing me to the shivering, vulnerable mass of jelly I am underneath.

"Yeah…" I nod, feeling my teeth start to chatter in time to my head-nodding.

"C'mere," he motions to me, leaning over to switch on the small convector heater in Sarah's room.

Instant warmth – in two ways. How can I refuse? Even if shyness is practically paralysing every stilted step I take towards him.

"You and Sarah," he smiles at me as I crouch down in front of the heater and, coincidentally, at his feet, "do you always bicker like that?"

He's got a very fine silver chain around his neck, I notice. Whatever's on the end of it is unseen, hidden behind the neck of his dark-blue top. Has Sarah seen it at close quarters...?

"Hey, what can I say?" I shrug, not looking him in the eye.

And what *can* I say? "See that beautiful, talented, exciting girl you're going out with? Well, you *do* realise she's a manipulating bitch, don't you?" Hey, it may be the truth, but while his vision is currently (unfortunately) clouded by the rose petals of romance when it comes to my sister, it's easier to be vague.

"I know what it's like. Me and my big brother fought like crazy till he went away to university. Best thing that ever happened to us – now I have a great time when I go to visit him, and we always go out together when he's home. Before last summer, we'd have been more likely to kick each other's heads in than go for a pint together!"

I realise what he's trying to do; he's trying to comfort me. Big wow. And I don't mean that sarcastically: no one in my family – Mum, Dad, Sarah – has ever tried to rationalise it; none of them has ever suggested that what goes on between me and Sarah is normal and will pass. That's because Mum and Dad keep their heads in the sand, and because what goes on between me and Sarah is anything *but* normal, even if it does seem like harmless bickering on the surface. Oh, no – I don't expect any cosy chats over a few glasses of wine in some student union in the future. The sooner me and Sarah have enough independence and money, I can guarantee that the two of us will keep as far apart from each other as the occasional enforced family get-together will allow.

"How old's your brother?" I ask, flicking a shy look Conor's way.

Worn, grey cord jeans, Kicker boots, fleece-lined denim jacket, dark-blue top, that glint of a chain at his neck, the floppy, slightly unwashed hair, a grin that brings his whole face to life, big, brown eyes with a fluttering of sandy lashes all around them. In the computerised filing section of my brain, it's all noted, all bookmarked.

"Twenty-one. Three years older than me. He's aiming to do a Masters degree in Financial Regulation and Compliance Management."

"Whatever *that* is," I hear myself saying as I start to thaw out in front of the heater.

"Exactly!" I hear Conor laughing and, self-consciously, I start laughing too, feeling slightly hysterical that I've inadvertently cracked a joke with the one person I'd wanted to make an impression on since the moment – freeze-framed for ever in my memory – that I saw him.

Of course it all gets ruined. It has to, doesn't it? Knowing *my* luck?

"Ready already?" Conor smiles at something over my shoulder. That something being Sarah. I turn and see she has red-rimmed eyes, probably from ramming her contact lenses in too quickly in her rush to get back here once she heard me and Conor talking.

Filthy.

That's the only word to describe the look Sarah gives me with her reddened eyes. But hey, what's new?

I stumble to my feet, and with a quick wave 'bye in Conor's direction, pad barefoot across the hall towards my own room, feeling the warmth of the heater and Conor's friendliness being replaced by icy prickles on my skin, courtesy of the wisps of draughts in our house and the frosty glare I can still feel emanating from my ice queen of a sister.

Chapter 5
Funny? Peculiar...

"You sat next to him, practically *naked*?!"

That's Pamela, whispering, even though the classroom is almost empty. I say almost: Miss Jamal, our English teacher, is in a bit of a huddle over at her desk with Mr Fisher, the music teacher. Wonder if there's anything going on with the two of them? Miss Jamal is kind of OK-looking and Mr Fisher is pretty cute for someone who must be about thirty, so it's not like it's a totally wild, out-of-the-question idea.

Hmm – and how would Sarah feel about that? I know she's seeing Conor, but ever since she first mentioned this Battle of the Bands stuff, it's been "Mr Fisher" this, and "Mr Fisher" that every five seconds. You know, it really wouldn't surprise me if she had a bit of a thing for him…

"Didn't you just want to *die* of embarrassment, Megan?!" Pamela gasps.

"I wasn't *naked*!" I whisper back, handing a pile of muddled textbooks down off the shelf to Pamela's waiting hands and peering out through the door of the walk-in cupboard at the two teachers. "I told you, I was wearing a *towel*!"

Me and Pamela are on volunteer tidying duty, spending our precious Monday morning break trying to make sense of the jumble on the shelves here. I really mean it about the volunteer bit; we haven't been forced into it and we're not complete mugs or anything, it's just that when you're a stunningly average student, teachers tend to give you a hard time. Unless, of course, you prove yourself to be an exceptionally accommodating and pleasant pupil. So when Miss Jamal asked for help with this deadly dull task, me and Pamela (my equally average accomplice) offered our services straight away. If earning Brownie points with your teacher gives you an easier ride, then hell: I say, go for it. (I did spot a 'How To Study Better Spell' in my new book yesterday, but as it involved geranium oil, a bird feather and a piece of coal – none of which I happened to have handy – I never got round to trying it out.)

"Yeah, OK, so you were wearing a towel, but *still*, Megan! Weren't you *mortified*?!"

"No," I shrug. "I wasn't. I know I should have been, and I know normally I absolutely *would* have been, but somehow... he just didn't make me feel uncomfortable."

It was true. However shy or weird I felt sitting with Conor for that little while on Saturday night, the one thing I didn't feel was awkward. Or embarrassed. It's like a miracle, really – normally, I hate my pear-shaped body so much that I'll wrap a huge beach towel around me when I go swimming and only drop it at the last minute when I get to the poolside. On holidays abroad, I'm happier in long shorts and T-shirts than the micro-bikinis Sarah flaunts herself in.

"But, my God," Pamela goggles her eyes at me. "Wearing next to nothing in front of someone you fancy... I'd just *die*!"

She's imagining herself and Tariq, I can tell. You know, I'm really beginning to wish I hadn't told Pamela about what happened on Saturday *or* that I fancied Conor in the first place. For a start, she's pissing me off by making the whole thing sound seedy, and second, I'm not doing it to titillate her and get her mind working overtime about being in the same situation with Tariq. As if *that's* ever going to happen. They've never even been in the same room alone together, never said anything apart from shy "hi"s (still!) to each other. I mean, there's something fundamentally nuts about flirting by text and then acting too timid to talk to each other in the (fully-clothed) flesh, isn't there? OK, so I'm no super-confident ladette, who has a posse of male buddies and would think nothing of asking a guy out – I'm just the exact, polar opposite. But even *I* know Pamela and Tariq are goofing around pathetically. She's in a win-win situation: she likes him and knows for a fact that he likes her, so what are they waiting for? Some kind of matchmaker, like they had in Victorian times – or like they have in arranged marriages – to formally introduce them? God, *I'm* going to have to end up doing it, aren't I...?

"Look, Pamela, me and Conor talking – it only lasted for about one minute, till my sister came scurrying in," I say to the top of my friend's bowed head. I try to bring her wandering mind back to the conversation by thunking a particularly huge pile of books down into her arms...

"*Oww!*"

"Oops! I'm sorry!" I gasp as Pamela clutches the top of her head and tries to rub the pain away with the palms of her hands.

"Are you OK in there?"

Close up, Mr Fisher has the look of an older David Beckham about him, but maybe that's just because he's got that Number One buzzcut that Beckham made famous once upon a time. Behind him, Miss Jamal frowns at Pamela's whimpering and at the scattering of books over the cracked lino floor.

"I dropped them... only she, um, didn't catch them," I mumble uselessly in explanation, scampering quickly down the stepladder and immediately crouching down to gather up the mess.

"Come out here where it's brighter, so I can check you haven't been cut," Miss Jamal motions to Pamela, who shuffles past me, her scuffed, black, school brogues sending textbooks skimming off to the farthest corner of the cupboard.

"It's like an episode of *Itchy and Scratchy* in here!" Mr Fisher says wryly, squatting down and helping me gather up everything. "What was going to happen next? Was Pamela going to hit you in the face with a giant frying pan?"

"No – I was going to hide a bomb in a copy of *David Copperfield* and then ask her to read it out loud to me while I ran away!"

Mr Fisher laughs and I get that same spine-tingling thrill as when Conor laughed out loud at something I said on Saturday night. People – *male* people – finding me funny; this is a real novelty. The only one who's ever found me remotely funny up till now is Pamela, and that's 'cause it's in her Best Friend contract. (Just like it's in the contract that I have to listen to endless tales of long-distance longing from *her*.)

It's fair to say that my family have never found me funny. You know how you get a certain feeling that people have a set opinion of you, and no matter what you do or don't do, they'll always think that way? Well, my family probably think I'm a lot of stuff: difficult, moody, psycho even (hey, don't forget the scars – *they* never let me), but I can safely say that it would never occur to them to find me remotely funny. Funny peculiar maybe, but funny ha ha? You've *got* to be kidding.

"Listen, I've got a bit of a problem…" says Mr Fisher, suddenly getting kind of serious on me.

It's on the tip of my tongue to say, "Well, shouldn't you see a doctor?" but I bite my lip and hold myself back; there's only so much fooling around you can do with a teacher, even one who laughs at your jokes.

Instead, I raise my eyebrows in what I hope comes across as an expression of intelligent questioning, but which probably looks more like the look on a bunny's face two seconds before the juggernaut splats it.

"You know this Battle of the Bands competition that's coming up?"

I nod. Of course I do. Haven't I been singing the words to Ash's *Girl from Mars* every spare minute of the day since it dawned on me that *that* was what Conor and Sarah were rehearsing together in her room on Saturday night?

"Well, there's only two weeks to go and there's a hell of a lot of work to do with the school band that's entering—"

Wow! You mean something involving my sister *isn't* gold-plated perfection?!

"—actually, it's more a case of sorting out everyone else, like the lads who are doing the lighting for them, and the crew in the art department who are supposed to be coming up with a backdrop..."

Whatever. But why exactly is he telling me all this? I don't think Mr Fisher even knows my name – he only joined Bakerfield at the end of last summer, long after I'd opted out of Music.

"Anyhow, the point is, it's like spinning plates, and I can't manage to coordinate everything, and put the band through their paces, all on my own. I need help."

"Oh," I mutter, open-mouthed, for lack of anything else to say. Now I must look like a cross between a startled bunny and a *cod*, for God's sake!

"Yeah, so I was having a moan to Miss Jamal about it just now, telling her that what I *really* need is a runner – someone to zoom around and help me sort everything out – and she suggested either you or…"

He's bumbling now, throwing a thumb over his shoulder in the direction of Pamela somewhere out there in the brightly-lit classroom. Told you he didn't know my – or my friend's – name.

"Pamela," I reply, helpfully filling in the blank. "And I'm Megan."

"Megan. Yes, of course," he grins, knowing he's been caught out. "Anyway, Miss Jamal said that you two are always very willing to offer your services, and usually—"

He glances around at the general untidiness swamping the floor.

"—very efficient. So what about it?"

"Um .. what?" I mumble, knowing *exactly* what he's saying but too stunned to believe what I'm hearing.

"What about helping me out? Being my runner? It means sitting in on every after-school and weekend rehearsal, and then coming to the Battle of the Bands competition too. You'd need the afternoon off school, but I'd sort that if you're up for it."

"I'm up for it," I mutter, hardly able to move the frozen muscles in my face to make the words come out.

He must take my lack of facial expression to mean I'm not keen.

"Are you sure? Because I can always ask Pamela — if she doesn't have permanent amnesia after these books scoring a direct hit on her head!"

"No!!" I squawk a little too loudly. "I mean, yes, I'd love to help out. And, um, my sister's actually in the band."

"Yeah? You mean... Sarah?" I see Mr Fisher frown, instantly ruling out Angel and Cherish as obvious relations and settling on Sarah by a process of elimination.

I can see he's struggling to see the resemblance. But I don't care. I'm not offended; I'm elated — already a change is happening in my life, and it seems to be a change of luck. OK, maybe that's not the exact change I wished for over my PJ Harvey plastic CD cover a couple of nights ago, but it'll *more* than do.

And who knows, maybe even *that* wish will come true too, if I keep positive (and keep *everything* crossed)...

Chapter 6

The surprise – make that shock – party

Mum and Dad dropped me and my overnight bag at Pamela's this morning, on their way to the train station to spend the weekend with Auntie Kelly and Uncle Jack. All I can say is, thank God there was a band rehearsal to disappear to this afternoon. Pamela is in some seriously weird, distant mood at the moment and is zero fun to be around. Must be all the unrequited love messing with her head, although she went ballistic at me this morning when I suggested that. Hope she's in a better frame of mind by the time I get back to hers. Which is pretty soon, unfortunately, seeing as the rehearsal has just finished...

Mr Fisher has darted off to talk to the lad in charge

of the mixing desk, and he's left me to check with everyone that they're free for the next band practice – the last band practice before the competition next Friday. Hey – an excuse to talk to Conor close up... *what* could be more brilliant? But first, I'll have to find him. All the gear is still on stage, but Conor, Salman and Sarah have wandered off somewhere. Still, I can start with Cherish and Angel, I decide, heading up the wooden stairs that leads to the stage.

"Um, hi..." I hear myself squeak apologetically.

God, I wish I didn't get so intimidated at the idea of talking to the two of them. My hand is shaking so much that I have to clutch my clipboard tight so it doesn't show. I know, I know, I *know* they're only human, like me. The trouble is, they're stupidly gorgeous and they're super-cool, *unlike* me.

And, from the way they're ignoring me, it's obvious that my squeak is inaudible to the ears of the stupidly gorgeous and super-cool.

"So, are— are you OK for Tuesday?" I ask, a little louder.

Cherish and Angel stop chatting to each other as they wind up their mike leads and stare at me as if I'm a total stranger who's just walked up to them and started talking in Ancient Greek.

You know, Alice Morgan in our year: well, her big brother plays in the reserves for our local football team. His mates – guys who play for the first team; guys who've been in the papers and on the telly – they've given her personal signed photographs and everything. Me: I can't even get my sister's mates to acknowledge my existence. How bizarre... I'm just a totally nobody to them.

"What?" shrugs Angel, her long, dark hair tumbling off her shoulders as she speaks.

"Mr Fisher – he wants to know if you're OK for rehearsals on Tuesday?" I rephrase my question.

"Oh, Tuesday! Yeah, sure!" Cherish nods, now that she and Angel have realised the question has come from someone who actually *matters* (ie, not me).

With relief, I see Conor come back on to the stage, flipping open the empty bass guitar case he's just collected from backstage.

"Fine," I mumble at Angel and Cherish, as I quickly put a tick beside their names and hurry off to someone who will hopefully treat me more like a member of the human race.

"Hey, Megan!" Conor beams, not letting me down.

"Hi!" I grin, basking gratefully in the warmth of his welcoming smile.

"So how did that sound today?"

"Good! It sounded... great!" I babble enthusiastically as he unplugs his bass from the amp and lays it tenderly in its case.

"So, looking forward to the party?" he glances up at me.

"What party?"

My heart instantly soars at the idea that there might be some sort of after-show do at the Battle of the Bands competition.

"At yours, of course! Tonight!" Conor laughs, probably marvelling at how stupendously dense I was being.

"I— I didn't know there was one," I blinked in shock.

Funny, isn't it? The only way my parents could relax and enjoy their night away from home was knowing that I wasn't in the house, getting up to whatever I might get up to (well, it saved them locking all the sharp objects away, I guess). It was OK for Sarah to be home alone, though. Oh yes: she's the responsible, dependable one out of the two of us. The daughter who can be trusted.

Ha.

You want a bet, Mum? Dad?

Maybe I was feeling a little sorry for myself, or maybe the injustice of it all got the better of me, but whatever, I suddenly felt tears prickle in my eyes. I wasn't deliberately looking for the sympathy vote, but I got it anyway, which was pretty nice.

"Sarah didn't *tell* you?" Conor frowned at me. "But you'd be there whatever, right?"

Was that a "Hope you'll be there" sort of statement? I thought anxiously, before I shook my head back into reality.

"No – I'm supposed to be staying over at my friend Pamela's..." I mumble.

As the frown on Conor's forehead deepens, my own heartrate rises rapidly under the full-on beam of those brown eyes close up...

I'd say Sarah was surprised to see me walk in the front door, but I guess her expression had more to do with shock.

"Listen," Sarah hisses, her perfectly made-up face all angular and contorted with anger. "You *don't* have to be here, Megan."

"Yeah?" I say, in a hopefully brave tone of voice as I try to hang my coat up on the crowded rack and dump my bag on the floor, "I think I *do*. I live here too or have you conveniently forgotten that?"

Stunned at me taking a stand against her, Sarah is (yesss!!) temporarily lost for words, which gives me a second to stare at her. She's used her hair straighteners, I notice – you can tell by the way her hair is glassy flat, flatter than blow-drying can ever get it. But the glossy surface of her chestnutty hair is vibrating, I notice, maybe with suppressed rage, or maybe because the music exploding from the living room is sending sonic sound-booms through the whole house. I can feel the deep vibration in my chest like regular, flat-handed slaps, and the floor is shaking under the very soles of my Cat boots. Sarah's wearing boots too – only they're high and pointy, worn with raspberry cord flares, a long-sleeved, lacy, cropped black top, with nails and lips painted to match the rich, rusty pink-red of her jeans.

Over Sarah's shoulder, through the throng of people chatting in the hall, I can see Cherish in the kitchen, throwing back her head and blasting the drooling fan club of boys circling her with a throaty, dirty laugh.

"Megan, you're supposed to be staying at Pamela's. That's what you promised Mum and Dad!" Sarah snaps at me, raising her voice now that an extra loud Limp Bizkit track's just come on.

"Yeah? Well, I remember *you* promising that you'd look after the house while they're away. So, what if I phone Mum at Auntie Kelly's right now and tell her you've invited most of the school round to ours for a party her and Dad know nothing about?!" I answer my sister back. "Mind you, I don't even *need* to tell her you're having a party – she'll hear it loud and clear down the phone!"

Sarah looks like she wants to slap me, but I get the feeling that that's not just 'cause I'm cramping her style by turning up here at the party I'm not meant to know about, never mind be invited to. It's also because I'm helping Mr Fisher out. It's because I've been at the last two rehearsals – on Thursday night and all day today – and she likes that not *one* little bit. You should have seen her face when I announced over tea on Monday night that I was going to be Mr Fisher's runner. While Mum and Dad were oohing and aahing in my direction (makes a change), Sarah stayed resolutely silent and stared down at the plate in front of her as if her half-eaten lasagne was hypnotising her or something.

For a girl who gets everything she wants, no questions asked, you'd think she could be generous enough to wish me well just *once*. But that isn't the way Sarah operates; she *likes* having the no-hoper sister – it makes her all the more diamond-bright by comparison.

Anyway, maybe it's true, what I thought before – about her having a thing for Mr Fisher. Up close, it certainly looked like I might be right. At Thursday's rehearsals, when I was up on the gantry giving Alex (the guy doing the lights), some feedback from Mr Fisher, I got a bird's-eye view of what was going on. As the band – still with no name – ran through their number, Sarah didn't take her eyes off Mr Fisher, who was sitting out front in the first row of the school hall. And as for *posing*, you've honestly never seen anything like it. Yeah, so Cherish and Angel were giving it big licks, doing this co-ordinated hip wiggle dance in between their backing vocals, but Sarah *really* thought she was something. She deliberately set her mike stand low, so that when she joined in with Cherish and Angel, she sang with her chin tilted down and her eyes raised, all Bambi-cutesy. Idly, I wondered if – like the rest of the male population of the world – Mr Fisher was about to fall under her spell and enrol in the Cult of Sarah, but no. I had to hide my giggles behind my clipboard when Mr Fisher bounded on stage at the end of the run-through and immediately grappled Sarah's mike up to the same level as Cherish and Angel's, telling my sister matter-of-factly that she'd find this new height much more comfortable. Great! A man with a mind of his own, resisting being suckered by Sarah.

Speaking of guys who are suckered by Sarah, I hung

around on the darkened gantry for longer than I needed to, just for the luxury of one long, unseen, uninterrupted look at Conor. He stood virtually motionless as he belted out lead vocals, with only a flick of the head or the tap of one desert boot toe on the stage as he kept time. One skinny arm cradled the neck of his bass, while the other stayed practically straight, picking out the deep, reverberating bassline in time with Salman's drumming in the background. Alex, the lighting guy, had the whole of the stage bathed in staccato blasts of red and green, but the one yellow spotlight on Conor was constant, making his fair hair seem blonder, sun-kissed glints of gold darting as he did his head flick thing, tantalising shimmers of light catching on the mysterious, thin chain around his neck.

But that was then and this is now.

"And how exactly did you find out about the party?" Sarah shrieks after me as I think better of leaving my bag in the hall and stomp up the stairs, weaving between can-holding, chattering couples, towards my own room.

"I heard about it at rehearsal this afternoon," I tell her over my shoulder, almost *tasting* how much fun it's going to be to say the next bit. "Conor told me."

Oh yes! Just as I expected. Her face falls and it's as if I've punched her in the stomach. I raise my hand from the banister and give her a cheeky wave of triumph, which immediately makes her purse her lips and turn away. Well, it doesn't hurt to let her catch a glimpse of my wrist while I'm doing that. It *is* the wrist with the worst scars, and just in case she feels like getting on her high horse with me about being here, it's time she had a reminder of what I've been through – and whose fault that was. Maybe Sarah didn't hold the actual knife, but the scars are all her work, sure as night follows day, sure as guys like Conor never fall for girls like me...

More's the pity.

There're a couple of girls hovering outside the bathroom, hammering on the door and asking if someone called Ellie is all right in there. Evidentally, she's not, as the sound of barfing makes pretty obvious. Bustling past them into my own room, I'm relieved about two things: first, that there's no one loitering in here – barfing or otherwise. Sarah seems to have made it the spill-over space from the oversubscribed coat rack downstairs, and that I can just about handle. The second thing I'm relieved about, I think to myself as I brush on some black mascara in the mirror, is that I didn't invite Pamela along with me tonight. With a bit more make-up on I can look passable at this party, but with Pamela in tow – gawping wide-eyed at the drinking, the smoking and the barfing that seems to be going on – it would have been a dead give-away that I'm the uncool little sister. (Not that I care too much – there's only one person here that I'm interested in impressing.)

And it's not just the cool/uncool factor of having Pamela around either – like I say, she's gone funny on me this week, and when I think about it more it's been ever since I told her that Mr Fisher asked me to help him out, so staying over at hers wasn't exactly something I was wildly looking forward to. (Although it took ages to get away tonight; her mum insisted I had tea with them at least, and then forced me to wait for ever for Pamela's dad to drive me over here.)

Great, isn't it? I can't even rely on my best friend to be chuffed for me, to be pleased that for once something's going right for me, without jealousy clouding everything. (At least that's what I *think* her problem is.) And another thing: I know for a *fact* that she holds me personally responsible for scaring Tariq off. As *if...* I thought I was doing her – and him – a favour by having a quiet little word in his ear last Tuesday; thought it would help speed things up a bit in the romance department. Wrong. Instead, he went silent on her – well, more silent than ever – letting her text messages drift unanswered in cyberspace, acting like he was fascinated by the dinner hall curtains whenever we've seen him since. What's that phrase? Shoot the messenger. Yeah, that's it. I mean, it's not *my* fault that Tariq's blown cold, just like it isn't *my* fault that Mr Fisher chose me to help him out, or that Conor spilled Sarah's little secret to me about the party tonight. But from the dirty looks I've had from my so-called best friend and my stupid sister lately, you'd think *I* was the bad guy.

Well, I'm sorry, but I'm *not* the bad guy, and if I can, I'm going to have as good a time as you can when you're at a party you not only haven't been invited to but aren't remotely welcome at either.

I tuck my conditioner-resistant frizz of hair behind my ears and head out on to the first floor landing, where there's now no sign of Ellie the Puker or her friends (though I'm not about to check out what state the bathroom's in right now). I put my hand on the banister, take a deep breath and get ready to head downstairs when I hear a sound, a sound that makes the hairs on my neck prickle with embarrassment – and it's coming from Sarah's room.

I've never heard anyone have sex before.

In the movies, yeah – of *course* there's always plenty of rolling-around-in-crisp-white-sheets action going on, with accompanying moans and groans of passion. But this – this *has* to be the real thing, right? And I don't know whether to be shocked or get the giggles. No, actually, I'm shocked: I dart away from the sliver of open door I'm peeking through as if my eyeball's just been seared by a blowtorch. That... that's *definitely* Angel in there, doing something X-rated with someone I can't make out because it's too dark. God, I kind of wish Pamela *was* here now, so I could have someone to gasp over this with.

I back away quickly, feeling dirty and soiled, even though *I'm* not the one doing anything to be ashamed of. You know, I'd never admit it to my sister but I've always been in total awe of her mates, but what Angel is getting up to in there is so seedy, fumbling away half-undressed in a room where anyone could walk in on her, even if they're only just stumbling around in search of the loo. What happened to stupidly gorgeous, to super-cool?

God, Angel's as ordinary and dumb as the rest of us. And what she's up to right now – I can't think of anything more nasty and less sexy...

Unless it's Sarah doing the same thing.

Near enough.

Well, from where I'm now standing at the top of the stairs, it looks like Sarah's flirting for Britain down there in the living room doorway; her lacy black top is slipping off one shoulder, her obviously braless boobs are jiggling under the thin material as she laughs. Hey, maybe she's planning on following in Angel's footsteps any time now...

Wonder what Conor would think if he could see what she was up to with this guy? I muse, hunkering down on the top step of the staircase, receding into the shadows and studying what exactly my sister's up to.

And I'm particularly intrigued by what Conor would make of it, since the guy presently drooling over Sarah's mating display isn't him.

Then I spot it: Conor's face – freeze-framed in shock – in the crowded living room, just beyond an unaware (uncaring?) Sarah and her new love interest.

"Oh, Conor... you picked the wrong sister," I whisper under my breath, knowing that he'll never hear those words come from my mouth, and sadly, would never believe them if he did...

Chapter 7
A secret shared...

"Here, brought you a coffee, Pumpkin. And a couple of biscuits," Mum beams at me as she backs into the boxroom with a tray. (Dad likes to call this the study. Pretentious or what? OK, so it's got a desk and a computer in it, but considering the rest of the small space is taken up with golf clubs, boxes that are full of stuff no one can remember and assorted furniture that's migrated from other rooms, I'd definitely just call it a bog-standard boxroom.)

"Thanks, Mum," I smile back, moving my homework over a little to make space for the tray.

It's the first time I've seen her smile since her and Dad got back late this afternoon and saw the state of the place. It didn't matter how much Shake'n'Vac Sarah threw down in front of the hoover, or how much air freshener she wafted around, it was impossible to really hide the stench of beer-soaked carpets or get rid of the haze of smoke that was clinging to everything (and still is). It's funny, isn't it? How parties can look vaguely glamorous when there's crowds and noise and low lights, I mean. But under the cold, accusing glare of a hundred watt bulb, once there's nothing left to see but five black bin liners-worth of disgusting fag ends and beer-can detritus to clear up, it's got all the glamour and allure of a multi-storey car park.

Since half nine last night, when I saw Conor grab his coat and storm out, I've spent most of the time in my room. As soon as I saw him slam the front door, that was it for me; the idea of escaping to my own little haven (complete with a chair jamming the door shut) was infinitely better then hanging around with all the drunken drongos cluttering up my house, now that the *one* decent person had left. Today, I slept late, since the music and noise and thoughts of what exactly had gone on between Conor and Sarah kept me tossing and turning till the early hours. When I *did* finally pad my way downstairs and saw what a disaster zone the place had turned into overnight, well, it's safe to say I made up my mind that

Sarah could count me out on the great cover-up front (actually, she didn't dare *ask*), so I left her and the hoover to it and holed up in my room with a tuna sandwich and a couple of Cokes. Then, when my traumatised parents were going ballistic at her during the last few hours, I made sure I stayed well and truly hidden in my room. I'm not some vindictive ghoul; I didn't *need* to hear them tearing into her. I was happy enough just revelling in the good sister role for once in my life. And while my mum and dad still seemed to assume I'd stuck to the plan and stayed over at Pamela's, I wasn't about to set them straight.

"It hasn't upset you, all this nonsense with Sarah today, has it?" Mum gazes down at me, crinkling her neatly plucked eyebrows in concern.

"No," I shake my head. "I'm just glad that nobody did anything to my room, that's all."

"I know, I know..." Mum pats me on the shoulder. "Well, Sarah *has* been a very silly girl for letting it happen. I suppose she was led astray by Cherish and Angel – she said they were the ones who persuaded her to have the stupid party in the first place..."

I don't mean to have any particular expression on my face, but Mum spots it straight away.

"I know... I *know* I shouldn't make excuses for her,

Megan," Mum bites her lip, chastised by my look, a cynical, disbelieving "Oh, *yeah*?!" if it conveyed what I was thinking.deep-down "So... you won't be working too late on your homework, will you, Meg?"

"Just got a bit more to do," I tell her, tapping on the scribbled papers by my side.

"Good for you. But when you finish, why don't you come down and join your dad and me? *When Harry Met Sally* is coming on soon..."

Wow. I feel like the Chosen One. (Sarah, the usual Chosen One, is currently squirrelled away in her room, licking her wounds.) Just like my tarot cards said, things *are* changing, and *fast*.

"By the way, I forgot to tell you," says Mum, halfway out the door then peeking back round it again. "When we got back this afternoon, old Mrs Harrison was sweeping her path and called me over. She said you'd helped her last week – lifting a cupboard or something?"

"Bookshelves," I correct her.

"Bookshelves then. You know, that was really, *really* kind of you, Megan. Why didn't you tell us about it?"

I shrug and feel myself blushing slightly at her words. But how can I answer her truthfully? How can I tell her that the reason I kept quiet was because I can never normally get a word in edgeways when we're all together, since the conversation (and the world) revolves around Sarah?

"Well, your dad and I are very proud, Pumpkin."

For once, I don't hate being called Pumpkin; I'm too stunned at the compliments I'm hearing. I'm also glad when I see Mum retreat from the doorway and shut the door behind her, before she can see the grateful tears that are trembling, on the verge of tumbling, from my eyes.

I have to do something fast to take my mind off this. Blindly, I turn back to the screen and hesitantly double-click on what I *think* is my homework essay. Instead, what flashes up is something completely different. I don't know how I managed it, but I've just opened up an e-mail – and an e-mail to Sarah from her friend Angel. It's dated today, 2.27pm to be precise; I spot that just as I'm about to close the file and try again. And then my finger stalls, hovering over the mouse, not quite connecting my finger with the clicker, not quite doing what I thought I'd do. This is awful… it's private… I shouldn't be looking, but I can't stop myself.

Omigod, I can't believe I got that drunk last night. I feel such a fool, Sarah – a total, complete idiot. Yeah, you were right when you asked if I'd done it with Joel last night. I'm sorry if I got angry with you and tried to deny it – I was just off my face. And off my head for – oh, I can't even believe it happened – losing my virginity to that big-headed creep!

I feel dizzy as I read, and then realise I'm so stunned I've forgotten to breath. I take a deep gasp of air and carry on where I left off, even though I feel swamped in guilt, like I'm scanning through someone's diary.

And he is a creep. You know how dumb I am? Before he shot off, without even saying goodbye, I asked him if it meant we were going out now. And he just laughed in my face! Can you believe it?! But what am I going to do, Sarah? I could be pregnant or anything! I know you can get the morning-after pill, but this is Sunday, for God's sake. Don't suppose they do a morning-after-the-morning-after pill, do they? Uhhhh... I know I sound like I'm joking around about it, but I'm not. I'm desperate, I've got tears streaming down my face as I write this. I feel like killing myself – I'm not kidding. I feel like going up to the bridge over the bypass and chucking myself off in front of the first lorry I see.

What am I going to do?

Please write back, babes (don't phone me – I can't talk about this with my family kicking around, obviously).

And please, please, please, I beg you, don't tell anyone else about this – not even Cherish. I couldn't stand the shame.

Angel xxx

My head and my heart are pounding. Poor Angel – last night I was disgusted by her, and today I feel as sorry as I did for Conor when I saw Sarah doing her flirt routine. Maybe Sarah should go out with this Joel guy. He sounds as despicable as *her...*

You know, I should exit this stuff, but I'm too far in now – I really need to know what advice Sarah ended up giving Angel (my mind boggles). I open up the Sent box and see an e-mail from Sarah, sent earlier today. But it's not directed to Angel – the name coming up is Cherish. My stomach in my mouth, I double-click, and find myself staring at Angel's cut-and-copied cry for help.

"The bitch!" I mumble, hardly able to believe that my sister could be that callous. What's the deal with her? Was it just too good a piece of gossip to keep to herself, like Angel begged her to do? Is Sarah getting off on the fact that Angel's messed up so badly?

Suddenly, I jerk in shock – that's Sarah's door

clicking open. Hurriedly, fingers shaking, I quit the e-mails.

"Oh."

That's Sarah, peering around the door and staring at me with zilch expression on her face. Her eyes are red, though – looks like she's been crying. Wonder if that's because of the humiliation of getting a bollocking from Mum and Dad, or about whatever went on between her and Conor last night? Who cares? She *deserves* to be miserable.

"What?" I say, hoping my voice isn't as wobbly as I feel right now.

"Are you going to be on the computer long?" she asks me flatly. "There's something I've forgotten to do."

What? Send copies of Angel's e-mail to everyone else in your address book for a laugh? I think, but don't say.

"I'm finished now," I shrug, getting to my feet and scrabbling my papers up from the side of my untouched tray of coffee and biscuits.

I breathe myself flat, slithering paper-thin past Sarah without touching her. She's been a two-timing cow where Conor's concerned and a treacherous one to Angel. Underneath all that fake niceness, she's just callous, there's no other word for it. And you know, it brings it all back to me, the way she walked out of the room that day; that day last summer when I got back from the hospital. She didn't even have the decency to ask how I was. Oh, yes, I don't want to be within spitting distance of Sarah.

Though right now, that's exactly what I'd like to do to her.

Chapter 8
On the Angel trail

Um... I'm not a musician, but from where I'm standing, it sounds to me like Salman is drumming along to a *totally* different track to the one the others are thrashing through. Conor's bass-playing doesn't sound quite right either, and on closer inspection, I see that one of the thick, metal strings on his guitar has snapped and is flapping wildly around, in danger of taking an eye out. Sarah and Cherish: their backing vocals aren't up to much, partly I think because Cherish seems to be trying to out-harmonise Sarah and partly because Angel is... well, Angel isn't around.

Finally, the band's version of *Girl from Mars* – which the original band would be hard pushed to recognise from that performance – grinds to a halt, with Salman managing to finish a few seconds ahead of anyone else. Oops.

A drumstick, chucked in anger by Sal, skitters along the wooden floor of the stage and slaps Cherish on the ankle. I watch her turn and glower at Salman, but that's nothing new. This Tuesday night's rehearsal has been a ramshackle mess of bad performances and bad vibes since the start.

"And we're *not* calling ourselves 'Angelic'," I can just make out Salman muttering blackly.

"*What* did you say?" Cherish storms over towards him. "Do you want to say something, Sal?! 'Cause if you do, there's no point mumbling, like a pissed-off, six-year-old kid!"

"I *said*," Salman roars, extra loud, "we're *not* calling ourselves 'Angelic'! *Right*?!"

"You got a better idea then?" Cherish challenges him. "'Cause we've been through lists and lists of stupid names for the band and all *you* can do is moan about them. Not once, not *once*, have I heard you come up with anything constructive!"

"You're just on your high horse 'cause I said no to calling ourselves after *you*, Miss I-want-to-be-a-star!!"

"Listen, I did *not* suggest 'Cherish' as a band name

– Sarah did! So don't you *dare* start yelling at me about that!"

Sarah, I notice, isn't even looking at them; she's hauling her guitar off and heading over towards an amp at the side of the stage.

"I'm not the *only* one who doesn't want a poxy, girly name for the band!" Salman barks at Cherish. "Ask *him*! Ask Conor! *You* don't want to go out in front of all these other schools with a name like 'Angelic' or 'Cherish', do you? We'll get laughed off stage!"

"I don't care," Conor shrugs.

"Well, you *should* care!" Cherish rounds on him now. "What's the point in entering this damn thing if you're the lead singer and you don't even care?!"

"That's what I'm asking myself!" Conor snaps back at her, dropping down on to his knees and furiously twisting the machine-heads holding his broken string in place.

Then suddenly they're all silent, the storm that whisked up so quickly between them now abating to stony sulks.

"For God's sake!" I hear a weary sigh close beside me.

Ben is losing it. That's Mr Fisher to you – *and* me. I just get a certain thrill using his name in my head, since I spotted it in his Filofax when he was flicking through it next to me during one rehearsal. I know it's crazy, but it's always somehow strangely surprising when you find out that a teacher has a first name.

"Er… anything I can help with?" I ask tentatively, as Ben leans forward in his chair, sticking his elbows on his knees and rubbing his hands agitatedly over his head.

I'm not sure whether to sit down next to him in the row (too matey?) or keep standing (more professional?). In the end, I compromise and perch my bum on the back of the row of seats in front, with my back to the stage and the non-speaking band.

For a second, Ben says nothing and I find myself agitatedly drumming my fingernails on the clipboard and notes that go everywhere with me these days, and stare down at the top of his head, where, I notice, there is a large, hairless, pink patch. Ah… so *that's* why he goes for the to-the-bone crop. It's *not* a fashion statement, it's to hide his failing follicles. *How* funny. And how sad that Sarah can have a bit of a crush on someone going bald! God, the girl's got no taste. She had Conor on a plate, but she prefers drooling over old guys and flirting with strangers at parties while the cutest, coolest guy slips right through her fingers. And speaking of Sarah and the boy she let slip away, since the start of rehearsal they have been doing a whole lot of ignoring each other, which adds that *extra* edge of tension up there on stage.

"Well, Megan, let's see," says Ben wryly, straightening up and looking me square in the eye. "If you happen to know a quick cure for flu so Alex is able to do the lights on Friday; if you can put a rocket under the art department and get them to deliver the backdrop they've been promising for the last two weeks; if you can work out how to get this lot to play properly and stop arguing for five minutes *and* decide on a name so I can phone it through to the Battle of the Bands organisers in time for them to put it on the damn *programme*, then *that* would make my life a lot easier. Oh, and Angel seems to have gone AWOL for the last twenty minutes, so if you can locate her too, that would be rather nice."

He's frustrated, but he's funny, I'll give him that. Wish more of the teachers at Bakerfield were like that, instead of having sense-of-humour bypasses.

"Listen, B— Mr Fisher," I begin, nearly slipping into that danger zone of thinking of him as a friend rather than a teacher. "Give me Alex's number and I'll phone him at home and see how he's doing. And tomorrow at school, I'll track down the art lot and find out what's going on. I can't do anything about the way the band are playing, but about the name – why don't *you* just choose it, since they can't make up their minds? And Angel…

I'm on to it. I'll go and hunt for her right now, if you like."

"I like!" Ben laughs. "Megan, you're a marvel! How could I have got through all this without you?"

He can't see, but my nails are digging deep into the palms of my hands as I clench them, trying hard not to tremble at the thrill of the compliment. A girl could get dizzy with all this; it's been total niceness overkill at home too, with Mum and Dad dishing the smiles and compliments in my direction every time I lift a finger and even when I don't. I tell you, Sarah should mess up more often – it makes my life *so* much more fun.

"Better get on the Angel trail then!" I smile shyly at Ben and shuffle off.

Briefly, I gaze at the stage and the four people on it who are resolutely not talking to each other. Conor has his head down, busily fixing the string on his bass. Salman is sitting brooding, arms folded, behind his kit, looking like he'd cheerfully chuck his other drumstick at the next person who opens their mouth (Cherish better keep her big trap shut). Speaking of Cherish, she's examining her nails and Sarah is slumped on the amp now, both hands clutching the neck of her guitar, as if she was holding on to it to save herself from drowning.

Honestly, this lot will have to get it together or they might as well forget about Friday. And whatever I feel about Sarah, call me selfish, but I don't want anything to mess up their chances at the competition – I've never been involved in anything this exciting, and I don't want it to be over before it's begun. *Please...*

I should star in the next *Lethal Weapon* movie, thanks to my amazing detective skills.

OK, it wasn't *that* hard to work out where an upset girl would go, and when I didn't find Angel in the backstage loos, I headed straight for the main girls' toilets in the corridor outside the school hall.

And it wasn't as if I had to follow the racking sounds of sobs to a lone cubicle, where Angel was hunched inside, inconsolable; nothing *like* that dramatic. It was just a case of finding Angel here, leaning on a pearly-white sink, staring miserably at her reflection in the mirror.

What was she searching for? Any tell-tale, outward signs that would give away what she did on Saturday night?

"Bog off," she says wearily, staring at me in the mirror.

She has her long, straight mane of dark hair tied back off her face tonight, pulled into a stern, single plait that trails limply down her back. It might not be her usual catwalk model/sex kitten style but she still looks amazing, specially now the sheets of hair aren't hiding her feline eyes and cheekbones.

"Mr Fisher... he was wondering where you were," I mumble, suddenly feeling once again like Sarah's gawky little sister and not Ben's efficient PA under Angel's disparaging gaze. And I resent that, just like I resent Pamela still acting all petulant and moody on me this week. It's time I left all that juvenile behaviour and feelings behind. If things are changing for me, then it's time I changed myself too.

"So?" Angel shrugs, willing me to sod off with her hooded-eye glare.

Angry bubbles of resentment froth in my chest, leaving me with a bitter taste on my tongue. I felt awful for Angel when I read her e-mail on Sunday, but it's hard to feel sorry for her when she's talking to me like I'm a lower life form than an amoeba.

"I know what happened at the party," I hear myself tell her calmly.

Angel frowns at me, not sure what I'm saying; not sure if her sleazy secret is safe or not.

Hey, guess what, Angel – it's not.

"I read what you wrote to Sarah," I carry on. Something stops me from announcing that I saw her and Joel... *together* in Sarah's room; maybe it's that old shoot-the-messenger thing. If I say I watched Angel through the crack in the door, I come out looking like I was spying on her, doing the whole peepshow routine. If I miss that bit out and go straight to Sarah's part in all this, then I come out smelling sweeter, if you see what I mean.

"And how *exactly* did you see what I wrote to Sarah?" Angel growls, turning away from the sink to face me. Her olive skin has turned grey and ashen, her eyes black and hard in her pale face.

"Sarah left it open on the computer we share. It was right in my face: I couldn't *help* seeing it," I reply, clutching my clipboard and taking a surreptitious deep breath to make myself stand taller.

"That was *private!*" Angel practically spits out.

"I'm— I'm sorry, but it can't have been *that* private," I hear myself ricochet back. "Y'see, the e-mail was from Sarah to Cherish. Your message just happened to be copied on to it!"

Angel has turned into a blur of blanched face and spinning, black plait pushing past me. There's nothing I can do apart from run behind her, watching her feet stamp with every hurried step along the polished lino corridor towards the hall. In my head, all I can make out is the thunder of my own feet, my own frantic heartbeat and breathless panting outracing them.

"You complete *cow*, Sarah Collins!" I hear Angel curse, before I barge my way through the still swinging double doors of the hall. "You think it's *funny* telling my business to the world? Like my life's some big *joke*?!"

I see Sarah now, still hunched on the amp, as Angel scrambles up the stairs at the side of the stage. She's got that expression on her face that I know so well – the Sweetpea face, the all-innocence face.

It's not doing anything for Angel.

"Hey, everyone!" Angel bellows at the top of her voice, throwing her arms out wide to an imaginary audience. "I LOST my VIRGINITY on Saturday!! Did everyone in town HEAR that? Or did you all get an E-MAIL about it from Sarah ALREADY?!"

Sarah sits open-mouthed, like she's watching a road traffic accident happen. Cherish has slapped her hands over her face and both the boys are gobsmacked. I swivel my head around quickly to see what Ben— Mr Fisher makes of all this, but he's nowhere to be seen.

"You mailed her message to other people? *Not* just me?!" Cherish stares hard at Sarah, dropping her hands from her face and thumping clenched fists on to her hips.

"No! No, I *didn't*! I only sent it to you, Cher! Honestly!" Sarah whines.

I always think of Sarah as model-tall and confident, but right now there's no smug smile of confidence on her face and it's as if she's shrinking under the shocked and disapproving gaze of the rest of the band – including Conor, who looks like he feels nothing but disgust for my sister, and maybe for himself for falling for her in the first place...

"It doesn't matter *how* many people you told, Sarah!" Angel starts sobbing angrily. "Don't you get it? I asked you, I *begged* you not to tell anyone else!"

"She's right! If she didn't want anyone else to know, then you shouldn't have told me!" Cherish snarls at Sarah, going over and wrapping her arms around a jerkily crumbling Angel.

I hadn't noticed up till this second, but Salman has come out from behind his drum kit and walked round to stand supportively close to Angel and Cherish, which is pretty funny, really, considering he seemed just about ready to bash out a drum roll on Cherish's head a few minutes ago. And even Conor has taken a few steps closer to Angel and co.

Sarah, on the far edge of the stage, is shrinking away in front of my very eyes, as if she's drunk from *Alice in Wonderland*'s bottle and begun shrivelling to a shadow of her former irresistible self.

Weird. I'm watching these four people gang up on my sister; I can almost feel the waves of hostility from down here, in the darkened auditorium. How surreal – usually it's a case of fans being trampled in the rush to fawn at Sarah's feet. Should I say something? Stand up for her? The second I think of blood being thicker than water, I realise that I'm scratching at my right wrist, worrying the white bumps of healed skin with sharp, tearing nails.

Sarah, I think, is on her own...

"I was only trying to help, Angel! I didn't know what to say to you! I thought Cherish might..." Sarah's protestations slip-slide away in the face of blank, accusing looks.

Suddenly, she gets to her feet, letting her guitar fall to the stage floor with an agonised twang of strings.

"Fine. Believe what you want to believe," she says in a shaky voice. "I quit."

"Oh, *great!*" Mr Fisher's voice booms down angrily in the darkness from the lighting gantry, as Sarah vanishes behind the black-out curtains backstage. "And what are we supposed to do *now?*"

What I'm going to do now is fumble for a seat in the gloom – I feel oddly light-headed and weak after witnessing that little scenario.

I'm catching my breath, trying to get the shivers to

subside when I see Conor staring down into the darkness, searching for something or someone.

As his eyes settle on me, holding my gaze for an endless few seconds, few moments, few minutes, hours, days, weeks, whatever, I forget to breathe and get the shivers back twice as bad...

Chapter 9

Take a chance on me...

"Oooh-ooooh-ooh-ah-ooh, babeeeeeeeee!"

An under-ten football tournament – that was the last thing the Forestdean Arena hosted. And this afternoon – in an hour to be precise – it's the turn of the Battle of the Bands competition. It's already mobbed in here and that's before the audience has been shipped in from the various schools taking part: band members, *friends* of band members, harassed competition organisers, stressed music teachers... they're all milling around the auditorium and the two temporary stages as singers take turns warbling through their songs while lighting and sound engineers twiddle knobs and buttons and shout frantically into headset mikes.

While the organised mayhem swirls by, I've parked myself on a plastic seat at the edge of Stage 2. Now that my lot have already sound-checked, this is a great spot for people-watching, and the people I'm currently watching are the lace-collared goth band from Market Hall School (called Velvet Death, for God's sake). They're distracting themselves from approaching stage fright by scowling menacingly at the wannabe R&B girl group from St Thomas's (Caramel), who are warming up their vocals on Stage 1. I don't mean to be cruel, but I think it's going to take a flame-thrower pointed at those girls for that to happen – their 'harmonies' are enough to make your ears bleed.

Speaking of flame-throwers, I could do with one now, to heat me up. This gaff is the size of an aircraft hangar and about as cosy. And then, if I wasn't cold enough already, I hear something that makes me freeze.

"Listen – it's like I *told* you, Mr Fisher! She can do it!"

"Now, come on; you don't know that, Conor."

"But I do – I've *heard* her. She sings along all the time, backstage, *and* she sounds as if she could harmonise just as well as Sarah. Actually, close your eyes and it could be Sarah singing!"

Instinctively, I throw the hood of my fleece over my

head and huddle down into its cosiness. But I'm not just doing this to keep warm; I'm trying to make myself disappear. If I try and move away, it'll be obvious to Mr Fisher and Conor – who must be standing practically behind me – that I'm here, within listening distance of their conversation. So I reckon it's better if I just stay put and try to think myself invisible.

"I don't know, Conor…"

"Look, *you* know and *I* know that it just doesn't sound strong enough with only Cherish and Angel doing backing vocals. We definitely need that third voice!"

"But it's a lot to ask of her. And it's all a bit last-minute."

As I listen in hard, I absent-mindedly doodle circles round the names Geeta, Neil and Omar on the sheet of paper on my clipboard. I flick my eyes up from the scrawl and see if I can actually see Geeta and the others: yep, over at the back of Stage 2, there they are, the so-called 'artists' working maniacally on the backdrop that they were meant to have finished weeks ago. The reason they're suddenly working so feverishly on it is that they decided at the last minute to add the band name on, since one had finally been chosen. Working on changes this late is kind of mad, if you ask me. But then they'd spotted the backdrop Dunmore School's entry had come up with – the name Seeker done out in tiny sparkles of light on a sheet of dense, black cloth – and panicked, I think.

"So what if it's last-minute? If it means the difference between standing a chance in this competition or not, then what's the problem?" Conor is arguing. "Anyway, it's our turn for a run-through in five minutes' time. We get her to rehearse with us then and if it doesn't work out, it doesn't work out. And if it does, well..."

"But how will Cherish and Angel feel?" Mr Fisher continues finding problems with Conor's suggestion.

"They want to win this thing as much as we do! Come on, Mr Fisher – let's find her and ask her!"

"She might say no, Conor."

Wrong, Mr Fisher; she might say yes.

God, am I acting really deluded here? It *is* me they're talking about, isn't it? I can't stand it any more, and spotting that the millions of members of the hip-hop band from Kendale School are just about to strut by, I swiftly stand up and duck behind them, using them as cover to walk *just* far enough away from Mr Fisher and Conor to pull my hood down, turn back and casually join them without either of them sussing that I'd been anywhere within earshot.

"Megan! Just the girl we wanted to see!" Mr Fisher beams at me.

I knew it, I knew it, I knew it...

How? Call me deluded (again), but I did another spell last night.

I know... I'm not really supposed to seriously believe in that stuff, am I? But this particular spell, I got it in my head to do it after the sort of *uncomfortable* few days I'd just had, what with Pamela now going icy cool on me at school, and Sarah giving me the silent, dead-eyed glare at home. It was a spell for confidence – ie, having some – and, I'm not kidding, after I did all the staring at the candlelight and spell recitation stuff, I could hardly *sleep* last night for this weird ball of excitement burning in my chest. Something good, something *amazing*, was going to happen today, for sure. I just hadn't known what it was until I'd overheard Conor and Mr Fisher just now.

"Megan, Conor and I have a big favour to ask of you..."

If Cherish and Angel had still been talking to Sarah, I guess their reaction towards me rehearsing with them would have been as frosty as if I'd landed on an iceberg wearing a bikini.

Instead, they'd just looked confused at this last-minute audition Mr Fisher had announced, which made the whole thing marginally less terrifying for me. (Only just.) I found that the only way to play it was not to look at the two girls; to stare straight out at the darkened hall, milling with rival bands and technicians, and do what I'd been doing in the privacy of my own room up till now, *and* backstage within Conor's hearing, even though I hadn't realised it.

"Good, good," Mr Fisher had nodded matter-of-factly, once we'd run through the song.

(Suddenly, my mouth felt cotton-wool dry with nerves. How had I just managed to sing?)

"See? I *told* you it would work!" I heard Conor shout triumphantly across the monitors at Mr Fisher, before turning and giving me a beaming smile and a big thumbs-up.

"That... that sounded great. I mean, together; we all sounded great," I suddenly heard Angel's voice say.

My God, she was talking to *me*.

"Yeah, it really did," I saw Cherish nod enthusiastically at Angel, then at me.

Wow – this felt like my own version of a fairy tale: Cinderella makes friends with the not-at-all-ugly sisters...

And three-quarters of an hour later, this Cinderella is about to see if the fairy tale is about to come crashing down around her ears. I mean, this is real now, this is it. I should be shaking, but weirdly, I'm not. I keep my eyes on Conor's back as he leads the way on to the stage, and find myself wondering what the strange, overwhelming roaring sound is. Then I realise it's the crowd from our school, cheering us on. Will Pamela be out there, do you think? She hadn't made up her mind to put her name down, last time I spoke to her, and since she hadn't been doing much speaking to me at all lately, I haven't a clue if her face will be out there, staring back in the darkness at us. I tell you, if sheer jealousy is what her stupid moods are all about, then seeing me standing on stage with Angel and Cherish and everyone is *really* going to do her head in...

For a split second, before I take my place at the mike, I see Salman settle himself behind the drum kit, the huge, spray-painted art backdrop behind that. Geeta and everyone might as well not have bothered spraying the name on (Near Miss, Mr Fisher had decided, after the band nearly broke up when Sarah walked out on them); it's impossible to read against the rest of the graffitied words and designs up there.

"Are you OK?" Angel squeezes my hand as we group around the back-up mike with Cherish.

A breathless "uh-huh" is all I manage to whisper back.

I'm OK, and this whole thing will be OK, I tell myself. I managed not to mess up the harmonies at our rushed, shoehorned-in, extra soundcheck earlier, didn't I?

"You look great!" Cherish mouths at me, looking pretty great herself, with her amazingly lush black curls glinting with a dusting of gold that she's also brushed over Angel's waterfall of hair and my own brown fizz of a hairdo.

Only it isn't really fizz any more, since Angel and Cherish got to work on me. I couldn't exactly claim to be the ugly duckling who turned into a beautiful swan, but I think I could pass for an almost cute duckling now, thanks to the hair-preening and make-up and the spare, black, stretch satin top of Angel's that I'm wearing.

Me, Cherish and Angel... who'd have thought?

Then Salman begins to tap out time on his drumsticks: here we go. I glance quickly at Mr Fisher, poised and ready to play Sarah's guitar part, and at Conor, who shoots me that look again – the fleeting glance that seems to have a chasm of meaning behind it.

I hadn't understood it the other night, when he'd stared down at me from the stage after Sarah stormed off. But I do now; crystal clear. Apart from humming along backstage, he'd heard me singing it in my room,

Conor said, the night we'd had the conversation in Sarah's room, right after she'd more or less banished me to my own bedroom.

Now... now this look is telling me that it's all right, he has confidence in me.

He needn't worry – for just about the first time in my life I have confidence in myself and it feels so mind-blowingly, heart-soaringly brilliant that it's all I can do to stop myself singing before my part actually begins.

Chapter 10
Luck... but which kind?

No wonder I need a minute alone, to take it all in.

What's it called again? The stuff that your body releases when you're happy? Endorphins, that's right. Well, it's been so long since I felt this happy that I'm feeling totally dizzy with this endorphin rush. My skin is still prickling with it; I'm so giddy I could giggle out loud.

Me. Second-best Megan. *I* just sang in front of four hundred people. *I* harmonised and did this brilliant little dance routine with two of the coolest girls in school, and I didn't mess up once. No one booed at me, no one laughed, no one told me I didn't fit in. It was *my* hand that Cherish held as we bounced down the steps of the stage afterwards, laughing with relief; it was *my* cheek that Angel kissed when we rushed off-stage, it was *me* who felt the warmth of that bear-hug from Conor...

But you know, for one second when I was singing, my confidence nearly slipped. I'm sure it was my imagination – it was too dark to make out any one person in the audience – but I was almost *positive* I saw Sarah out there, glowering at me, willing me to fail.

Just as quickly as that thought squeezed its way into my head, I told myself she'd never show up here today; never put herself through the humiliation of watching the band play without her. Her precious pride wouldn't let her.

But here comes someone I really do recognise, for real. Through the small crowd dancing in the middle of this huge, semi-darkened auditorium, I see a familiar figure wending his way carefully towards me, deftly moving from side to side whenever it looks like any of the dancers are about to barge into him.

"Brought you this," says Conor, handing me one of the two white plastic cups he's holding.

According to the teachers and the competition organisers, it's supposed to be a non-alcoholic punch-type thing, but *I* spotted the hip-hop band from Kendale pouring what looked suspiciously like a bottle of vodka into it earlier when the teachers and everyone were still trying to shoo the audience out to their waiting coaches so the after-show party proper could begin.

One bottle of vodka among this many people; it's not like it's exactly going to have that much effect. But then again, most of the members of Caramel are now treating Stage 1 like a giant podium, and by the looks of it, their music teacher's really having his eyes opened to the delights of butterfly dancing. (Not a pretty sight with the size of bums on a couple of those not particularly fly fly-girls.)

"Thanks," I smile shyly, now that I've used up most of my confidence reserves in the course of one rendition of *Girl from Mars*. Which won us second place, by the way; Velvet Death came first with an ultra-slow, gloom-drenched version of Madonna's *Like a Virgin*. "The judges liked the irony of it, I guess," Mr Fisher had shrugged, when the winner was announced. "It's a total fix," Salman had muttered darkly. "Did you check out that judge sitting in the middle? Old goth: no doubt about it."

I don't know whether Velvet Death won because they made the judges laugh, or whether the middle judge liked their lacy shirts, and I don't much care. All I know is that I got through something amazing today and I'm so proud I'm buzzing.

"So, Megan, what are you doing over here, all by yourself?" Conor asks, setting himself down beside me on the edge of Stage 2. "Angel was worried about you."

He has to bend close to speak to me, to be heard above the music belting out of the huge speakers. I feel the heat of his breath on my cheek and instant prickles at the back of my neck.

It's been an amazing couple of weeks, I whisper in my mind as my eyes run over Conor's face, memorising every eyelash, every smile line. *So many things have changed – I won't be the same again. Don't expect anything more…*

"Just wanted to get away on my own for a bit; take everything in," I shrug, taking a sip of my drink and trying not to wince at the initial sugary sweetness of it or the bitter alcohol kick behind that.

"I see," Conor smiles at me, nodding and looking suddenly shyer than I've seen him look. For a second, we both glance away from each other, both staring down into our non-alcoholic vodka cocktails.

Say something… the voice in my head bullies me. *Just 'cause I said you couldn't expect anything else, doesn't mean you should mess things up by going all goofy and silent on Conor.*

Spurred on, I'm just about to force myself to talk –

about the Caramel girls and their eye-popping hip-grinding, about the hip-hop guys' addition to the punch, about *anything* – when Conor gets in there before me.

"Can I ask you something?"

"Of course," I shrug.

Will you go out with me?

Will you run off to Mauritius with me and we'll get married under a dripping bower of bougainvillea? Or in Las Vegas with a singing Elvis as a witness if you like that idea better?

Will you have my babies? If we have a boy, we'll call him Kurt, after Kurt Cobain out of Nirvana; if it's a girl, Polly, in honour of the mighty rock chanteuse PJ (Polly Jean) Harvey, of course...

But I'm running ahead of myself, by about ten years, or ten *lifetimes*. The poor guy probably just wants to know the time...

Tentatively, Conor moves one hand from the worn corduroy of his jeaned thigh. For a moment, I think he's aiming to try and gently prise one of my hands away from the cup I'm clenching, and I can hardly breathe. But then his searching fingers stop at my wrist, slowly lifting the silky black material of my borrowed top away from my skin.

"I noticed the scars before, but I didn't like to ask..."

Gulp.

Where do I start? From the moment I realised that my big sister made me feel like shit? Do we really want to trudge back to my childhood of being made to feel second-best, second-rate, second-class? Or will I just cut to the chase and tell him about the night last summer when I'd had enough?

"It was Sarah's birthday," I lean close into Conor and begin to tell him. I have to be close for this private confession; up till now, only my family know the full story of what happened – everyone else, including Pamela, has an idea that once upon a time I tried to kill myself, but know better than to ask about it.

I feel him nod imperceptibly, his fair hair very slightly brushing my lips.

"My mum and dad – they took us out to this fancy restaurant, but I might as well not have bothered to go, they spent so much time talking to Sarah, hardly even noticing I was there. They hadn't *done* anything for *my* birthday a couple of months before that..."

I'm not touching him (I wish!) but I can feel his whole body tense up as I talk.

"Anyway, all through the meal, I'm feeling more and more down and my parents don't seem to notice they're treating me like I'm Cinderella or something, but why should they? That's the way it always is. But I know

Sarah gets what's going through my mind, 'cause every time my parents start praising her or whatever, she waits till they're looking the other way before she gives me these snidey little glances."

That felt like a shiver from Conor – but maybe the cold in the auditorium is seeping into his bones.

"So we get home and I just decided I'd had enough and went to my room. But Sarah hadn't had enough – she barges in, wafting the big cheque she's got off of Mum and Dad in my face, taped inside this card that says 'To our No. 1 daughter'. She really liked pointing that out to me."

I pause, feeling the choke in my throat at the memory of her flaunting that under my nose. I know I should have just told her to get a life, but after years of stuff like this, I suddenly... well, I guess I suddenly ran out of steam.

"You don't know what it's been like for years and years in my family, Conor... it's as if it all— I dunno. It's as if it all crowded in on me that one night."

I'm not sure if I can go on. But then I've come this far, and to be honest, with every sentence my long swallowed secret starts choking me that little bit less...

"What happened?" Conor asks softly.

"I waited till I thought they were all in bed, all asleep.

Then I went down to the kitchen and got a knife – I got a knife out of the drawer..."

I can't do it – I can't go on. I can't tell him about Mum finding me; about her trying desperately to bind my bleeding wrists with tea towels while she screamed for Dad to get us to the hospital; about seeing Sarah standing there on the stairs when the ambulance arrived, smiling her Sweetpea smile of total innocence...

"Megan," I hear Conor's voice somewhere above me and feel the electricity as his arm wraps around me.

But all too soon his comforting warmth is gone.

"Give me a couple of minutes. I promise, just two minutes. I'll be right back."

Oh yeah? I think to myself, feeling that beautifully warm arm peel Itself away from me, knowing I've frightened him off. God, how could I have landed all that on Conor and expected him to handle it? How can I expect him to understand a lifetime's worth of drip-drip torture adding up and adding up to one night of sheer, black, bottomless madness? He thinks I'm a freak now – some mad, overemotional girl who flipped out over nothing. Please, please, *please,* why didn't I just keep my mouth shut and my wrists covered...?

It's the end of the world... It's the end of the world... It's the end of the world... It's the end of the world... I whisper over and over again inside the private world of my whirling mind. It seems like that's a snatch of some forgotten lyric, but I can't remember – it's just how I feel right at this moment; the moment when I could forget all the fairy stories of spells and good fortune coming my way and realise that all I have to look forward to is a lifetime of luck, of the bad luck variety...

And then as the rocking I'm doing seems to be comforting me in some deep, dark way, a two-note guitar riff shoots insulin up my spinal cord.

Thank you, PJ Harvey; thank you, whoever's acting as DJ here: the irrepressible strains of PJ's *Good Fortune* blast out of the speakers, sending my heartache – and every hip-hop and R&B fan – shooting far away for one glorious, soul-enriching moment.

"Dance?" comes his voice, like the best dream I've ever had. The soundtrack to my life; the most gorgeous, glorious, good guy I've ever met sweeps me off my feet to the most gorgeous, glorious, feel-good rock track that's ever been recorded. "I requested this for you. I heard you playing it in your room a couple of times. You're really into her, aren't you?"

"Yes," I whisper to him, half-laughing, half-dying with relief that he's come back to me, and let myself drift weightless to my feet and into his arms.

Moving in slow, sensuous, on-the-spot circles among the other dancers, resting my head against Conor's strong, wiry chest, feeling the pressure of the chain around his neck on my temple, I know it can't get better than this.

Change...

Oh, yes it can.

Change...

Everyone's allowed to dream, aren't they?

Change...

A hand strokes the back of my neck while another holds me close around my waist. I've never felt this cared for, this loved. Oh, God, how can I even say that? I hardly know this boy. I hardly...

Too late. He's tilting my head up towards him; and now somehow his soft lips are on mine, a lifetime's sadness wiped out in one simple, skin-tingling kiss. I could melt away, slip softly between the floorboards like molten wax, but I won't. I want every cell in my body to remember this moment; the first moment in fourteen years-worth of memories when I felt like I mattered to someone.

A switch has just flipped in my head; I know, without spells or candles or tarot or PJ Harvey, that something had changed in my life tonight and there's no going back. I never have to live in anyone's shadow again.

Fingers crossed.

And currently, five of my fingers are crossing themselves around five of Conor's. That can only mean *double* good luck, can't it? And I think I might just deserve double helpings. Right?

So, wish me luck, if just this once...

PART TWO

Life in the light

Sarah's story

Chapter 1
Walking on eggshells

The ear-splitting wolf whistle practically makes me jump out of my skin.

"Hey, gorgeous, got a smile for us today?"

Before I know what I'm doing, I'm grinning at the builders, the very same builders who I've been studiously blanking for the last two weeks that they've been working on the empty house across the road from ours.

Those guys make me dread leaving the house every morning, having to run the gauntlet of all the whistling and catcalls. It's usually OK when I'm coming home from school 'cause it's winter and dark early so they're usually safely long gone. Not this evening though – this lot must have been working indoors, where chilly January winds won't whistle down their horrible builders' bum cleavages...

"Just ignore them, dear," old Mrs Harrison on the corner told me one morning when she saw me hurrying past her house with yelps of "Go on, show us your knickers, love!" ringing in my ears. Easy for Mrs Harrison to say; probably the last time anyone did that to *her* was sixty years ago. But then again, all the little kids round here love to buy into the idea that she's a witch: maybe I should ask her to do a spell to shut those creeps up. Or at least turn them into faintly attractive members of the human race, instead of the beer-bellied, mono-eyebrowed, loud-mouthed oiks that this lot are.

"Oooh – look at that, lads! We got a bit of a smile there! *Very* nice!"

Damn. Didn't really mean to waste any of my chirpy mood on them, but then again I'm practically bursting with my good news and I guess a little happiness slipped out without me meaning it to.

Hugging my fluffy coat around me, I turn gratefully into our path and see the cosy lights of the living room beckon. I can't wait to tell Mum and Dad; they'll be so excited for me. Specially Dad, since he used to be in a band himself in his younger days (yeah – like a couple of centuries ago!). Mum will be pleased because she just loves to hear good news, specially after the rocky time we've all had over the last few months.

Thinking that, I slow right down, feeling a heaviness sink on to my shoulders. Oh, please don't let Meg be in one of her moods…

"Hi!" I smile at everyone as I walk into the living room.

I'm glad I thought about Megan two seconds ago on the front step; it gave me a chance to take a deep breath and turn down my level of excitement. Being too bouncy seems to have a really bad effect on my sister; the happier any of us are, then this weird, inverse thing happens and she gets bluer and bluer right in front of our eyes.

"Hey, Sweetpea, what's with you?" Dad beams at me, sensing something's up, no matter how calm I'm pretending to be. "You look pleased with yourself!"

"Put your legs down, Pumpkin!" Mum orders Megan. "Let your sister sit down!"

Uh-oh – a glower from Megan. Better tread carefully.

"Nah, it's all right, Mum!" I smile and go to perch myself on the edge of her armchair.

"Don't be silly!" Mum smiles, putting a firm hand on the small of my back and propelling me towards the sofa and Megan. "Look – there's plenty of room over there!"

You know, I think Mum likes to try and push us

together – physically, if she can't manage emotionally – just in case Megan ever feels like opening up and talking to me. *That'll* be the day. I think there's more chance of Megan spilling the secrets of her troubled soul to the workmen across the street than talking to me.

I hover for a second as Megan makes a big drama of dragging her legs off the sofa, with a theatrical sigh. Her trainers have left a fine trail of dust and dirt on the sand-coloured sofa, I notice. Do I wipe that away before I sit down? Better not – she'll just take offence or something.

Honestly, the phrase walking on eggshells could have been invented for our family, and the way we have to act around Meg. She's always been touchy – even as a baby she'd yell if you looked at her the wrong way. And poor Mum and Dad: Christmas practically gave them ulcers. If Meg ever thought I'd ended up with a better present then her, then it would be day-long tears and tantrums. One year she went hysterical 'cause my brand-new Barbie was prettier than *her* brand-new Barbie – er, aren't they all exactly the same, with maybe different coloured plastic hair?

We've always made allowances for her ("she's just a delicate child," Nana used to say) but lately it's got a lot more stressful. Ever since—

"Come on then, Sarah! What's put that smile on your face?" Dad interrupts my thoughts, over the top of the sports pages of his newspaper.

Here goes.

Just tell them straight – no garbled babbling; nothing that could make Megan feel as if I'm flaunting anything in her face. Yeah, like I *would*. I'd do anything to protect my kid sister or to help her in any way, only I don't know how to. And if I did, I don't think she'd appreciate it one little bit.

"Well," I begin, shaking my coat off my shoulders now I realise that Mum's got the central heating pumping at Sahara desert temperatures, as usual.

"Oh, don't crush your new coat, darling!" Mum frowns at me. "Pumpkin – go and hang it up for your sister!"

God, I wish Mum wouldn't do that! She's always having these little whispered conversations with me and Dad about how fragile Megan's self-confidence is, how careful we have to be not to dent it. Then blam! – she's right in there with some dumb, thoughtless comment. I can feel Megan bristle beside me at Mum's order.

"No, it's fine! I'll hang it up in a minute myself!" I say cheerfully, but a sharp tug pulls the coat from my arms and Megan pads grumpily out of the room with it.

"Mum!" I mouth at her. "You shouldn't do that!"

Mum frowns, knowing she's goofed, and shoots a worried look at Dad, who shrugs sadly.

"Stop fussing, Angela!" Dad says out loud, trying hard to sound jovial, in the vague hope that the light-heartedness will transmit itself to Megan (no chance). "Let the girl talk!"

He gives me a wide-eyed nod. We're in this little conspiracy together, the three of us, trying hard to pretend for Megan's sake (and our own?) that everything is just hunky-dory.

"Well…" I begin, shooting a look outside to the hall, where Megan has disappeared with my coat. "Do you remember me mentioning the Battle of the Bands competition? The one I was in two minds about auditioning for?"

"Of course, yes!" Mum nods. "Was that where you were tonight? I thought you'd just gone round to Cherish's or Angel's."

"No – we all dared each other to go to the audition after school."

Me, Cherish and Angel – we do everything together. Even auditioning when we're all really scared of making fools of ourselves.

Only we didn't – make fools of ourselves, I mean. Not one bit.

"And what did that involve?" asks Dad, folding his paper away.

"Mr Fisher got us all to sing acapella for a couple of minutes – we got to choose whatever we wanted, so the three of us asked to do it together and we sang that old All Saints' song *Never Ever*."

"Ooh, lovely!" Mum nods encouragingly, although I don't think she really knows the song.

"Then Mr Fisher – my music teacher, remember? – he says, 'What about playing me a bit of guitar, Sarah?' and I nearly died. I mean, I haven't been learning all that long, so I never thought about trying out for that part in the band. But he wouldn't take no for an answer and just handed me a guitar and… and I just played a bit of this and a bit of that and he said, 'OK!'"

"OK what, exactly?" Mum asks, trying to understand what I'm saying.

"Well, Mr Fisher just said, 'I want you, Sarah!'"

God, that was funny. I couldn't *look* at Angel and Cherish when he came out with that particular statement – I knew they'd be doubled up with the giggles. 'I *want* you, Sarah!': it was like some terrible line out of a torrid romance novel. Still, I knew what he meant. He meant I was *in*. Half-an-hour before, I hadn't even been sure I was going to try out for the audition and now I wasn't just a backing singer, I was lead guitarist too.

Wow…

But I can't let out how 'wow' I feel inside – Megan has just walked back in and settled herself down on the arm of Mum's chair, rather than come and join me again on the sofa. She makes me feel like I'm contagious or something. I'm infected with the happiness bug, to which she is, of course, allergic...

"So, Mr Fisher chose you, out of *how* many people, Sarah?" Mum asks, wrapping an arm around Megan's waist, just to reassure her how special she is too.

"Well, there were about thirty people at the auditions today, and I think he saw more people yesterday, but I'm not sure exactly," I shrug as casually as I can. "But today he finally decided on which five to pick for the band line-up."

"And when is the actual Battle of the Bands competition happening?" Dad asks, shooting the tiniest of glances over towards Mum and Megan now, just to try and gauge the mood.

"A few weeks," I reply vaguely, since Megan's dull, dark gaze is making my happiness screw itself up into a tiny, tight ball that means precisely nothing.

"Who else is in the band with you? Did Cherish and Angel get picked?" Mum says next.

Then I spot what Megan's up to: scratching at her scars. She's not even doing it subtly – her scrabbling nails are millimetres from Mum's eyes. You know, I'd do anything to make things OK for Megan, but this really pisses me off. Whenever I've got anything to say, whenever Mum and Dad turn their attention to me for five seconds, Megan starts with the scratching, and always within Mum's eyeline.

What a coincidence. *Not.*

"Yeah... Cherish and Angel got picked too – they're doing backing vocals with me," I try to say conversationally, averting my eyes from what Megan's doing. "And there's this guy Conor who's going to play bass and sing too, and a lad called Salman who's going to be on drums. I *kind* of know both of them, but just to say hi to."

Conor and Salman... they're really cute. *Really* cute. I mean, before this audition, I used to stare at them (hey, make that *drool* at them) from afar, but close up, they're even cooler and funnier and nicer than I dared to think.

"And so what happens now?" Dad smiles a fake smile. I know he's desperate to make it seem like the real thing, but months and *years* of trying too hard for Megan's sake gives his enthusiasm a hollow ring.

"Well," I try to respond brightly, "we'll have to get together with Mr Fisher and work out what song we want to play, then it'll be a case of loads of rehearsals up until the competition!"

"Megan, don't do that!"

My heart sinks to somewhere around carpet level. Mum's spotted Megan's scratch-scratch routine finally.

"I've got homework," Megan mumbles in reply and disappears from the room in a cloud of gloom.

"Megan…!"

"Leave her!" Dad hisses at Mum.

"But maybe I should go to her!" Mum protests, her eyes filling with helpless tears.

"You know what Dr Glass said – we've got to give her time on her own, to work things out," Dad whispers to her.

"Let her stew in her own juice," I remember Granny saying one time, when a six-year-old Megan flipped out over some slight or another (she wasn't soft on Megan, not like Nana). I wish Granny was still alive. Maybe her down-to-earth views aren't too PC these days, but then again, maybe she could help us understand this human hurricane called Megan in our midst that *little* bit better…

For almost an hour we stare – the three of us – at a succession of stupid soaps and sitcoms on the telly, trying to drown out our collective misery at Megan's withdrawal by losing ourselves in a world of people with fictional problems.

Finally, when I feel my face ache with fake smiles, I

decide to call it a day.

"Better go do some practice then!" I laugh, and my parents give me their well-rehearsed laugh back.

With every step of the stairs, ever closer to my room, and Megan's too, I hear the dramatic dirge of PJ Harvey pound out. I used to like her, but Megan's obsession has made me come to associate everything she sings with misery. All I want to do is get into my own sweet room, close the door and play around on my long-neglected acoustic guitar for an hour or two; get my fingers fired up for what's to come.

How pathetic is this; to sink with my back against the door down on to my haunches, glad of this special little space that's all my own. Over there is my daisy-splattered duvet cover; a haze of pretty blue, gauzy curtain drapes over my window; my hi-fi and CD collection stand underneath the most beautiful print of Monet's 'Lilies' that makes me sigh with happiness every time I look at it, and then there's my precious guitar, standing in the corner...

Only it's not. It's lying flat on the floor, its strings facing towards the ceiling, something oddly out of place with it.

And then I see what it is: the neck; it's twisted and splintered. Oh my God... it's my fault. I propped it up against my desk, without even bothering to put it back in its case. My guitar wilted from neglect, shattering its frail neck as it fell.

A couple of hours ago, this had felt like a truly special day – a day with a midwinter rainbow hovering around – and now it feels like a disaster zone.

Hey, welcome to what it's like to be a member of the no-fun Collins family.

Chapter 2
Good times, bad vibes

As Conor bends slightly forward to fasten the clips on his guitar case, a chink of silver falls forward, swinging away from the taut skin of his neck. From it dangles a tiny, round something.

"What's that? A Saint Christopher?" I ask, reaching out and delicately holding the engraved disk before I realise what I'm doing.

God, how forward am I? OK, so we've been having a real laugh together during rehearsals – all five of us – but getting so close, so touchy-feely with Conor, is kind of overstepping the mark. Or maybe it just feels like that because I like him so much...

Am I blushing? I hope not, I hope not, I hope not.

"No," he replies, straightening up and reaching for the chain, just as I gingerly let go. "It's St Sebastian. St Sebastian of Aparicio, to be precise."

"I've never heard of him," I tell him. "I know St Christopher and St Francis of Assisi, but that's about it."

"Ooh, there're a lot of patron saints out there," Conor grins. "More than three thousand. And my gran is personally acquainted with all of them."

"Is she very religious?"

"Oh my God, yeah. And she'd shoot me if she heard me blaspheming like that," he jokes, making me relax again. "Her flat in Ireland, it's like a shrine to... well, *shrines.*"

"Wow..." I nod. "Is it a valuable collection?"

"Is it hell! It's all plastic! Plastic Madonna wall clocks; plastic Last Supper pictures with waterfall effects in the background; plastic baby Jesuses in glowing, neon cribs... Can you imagine the warehouse of the factory that makes that stuff? It must be like a cross between Heaven and Disneyland!"

He's got me giggling... but that probably has something to do with the nerves I feel whenever we're alone together, like now. Since they don't have any gear to pack away, Cherish and Angel zoomed off with a quick bye (and a knowing wink from Cherish, cheeky cow!) a few minutes ago. Salman's back in the rehearsal room, chatting to Mr Fisher. Me and Conor are out here by the equipment cupboard, which Conor has now disappeared into, stashing the bass guitar safely away.

"But go on – you never told me; who's St Sebastian?" I ask him, leaning on the door frame and watching him wrestle a bit of space among the jam of musical equipment. "What does he do exactly?"

"Patron saint of safe driving," mutters Conor, pausing to shoot a look over his shoulder.

Now I don't know whether to believe him or not.

"You're kidding, right?"

"Wrong," he laughs and stands upright, mission accomplished, bass stashed. "My gran sent me this chain the minute she heard I was taking driving lessons. Here, do you want me to pack your stuff away for you?"

He's pointing to the black guitar case and small amp on the floor next to me.

"No, it's all right – Mr Fisher's OK'd it for me to take this home to practise on. I still feel a little sticky with that middle eight part."

For the rehearsal and performance, I'll be using the school's electric guitar. I'd planned to fool around at home on my acoustic, but since that's currently in guitar hospital, it's lucky that Mr Fisher is fine about me taking school property off the premises. Apart from helping me learn my part better, it's also going to give me pretty impressive arm muscles, hiking *that* lot back and forth.

Conor's obviously thinking along similar lines, the way he's frowning at the gear.

"I just can't believe there's a patron saint of safe driving!" I hear myself twittering, getting a buzz from being so close to Conor and desperate for the conversation not to fizzle out.

"There's a patron saint of practically everything!" He grins his gorgeous grin at me. "Saint Isidore of Seville: she's the patron saint of the Internet and computers in general. Gran sent me a whole lot of bumph about her when my parents bought me my i-Mac. I tried praying to her when the thing kept crashing, but it didn't work. Still had to send it away to get fixed."

I should get Conor to ask his gran if there's a patron saint for stressed-out families, but I don't want to put a damper on a good time by bringing up the touchy topic of my sister.

"You know, my favourite patron saint *has* to be Guy of Andelecht," he continues, locking up the cupboard.

"Oh, yeah? And what does *he* do?" I ask, taking the opportunity, as Conor turns away from me, to ogle his very nice bum in his cute, faded brown cords.

"Patron saint of sheds," he laughs, spinning around to face me so quickly that he nearly catches me drooling at him like one of the workmen that hassle me every morning. "When Dad ordered a new shed for the garden, my gran was straight on the case, sending blessings from Saint Guy."

"God bless this shed and all who sail in her..." I feebly joke, but Conor seems to think that's funny.

Good grief, how glad am I that I went in for the audition at the last minute? I wouldn't have the competition to look forward to, I wouldn't have the rehearsals to look forward to, I wouldn't have these snatched, brilliant conversations with Conor to look forward to...

"Listen, hold on and I'll give the key to Mr Fisher. Then I'll give you a hand with that stuff."

My mind's all aflutter as he pads off along the corridor towards the rehearsal room. What does he mean, he'll give me a hand? A hand down the stairs? A hand out of the school? He can't mean all the way home, can he? Can he?

We've walked and talked for ages, making the twenty-minute trawl from school to my house stretch out to almost an hour.

At a couple of main junctions, manic Saturday afternoon traffic thunders by, but I hardly notice it. I'm so wrapped up in Conor that it's as if I'm watching it all at a distance, with the volume turned right down. Conor's been doing most of the talking, telling me about Salman and how they've been mates since primary school, but I've chipped in about my history with Cherish and Angel, how I got to be friends with them in Year 7 when they were being picked on by this racist pig Wayne Stevens (expelled for carrying a knife into school in Year 8). Conor talked about his hero, Jean-Jacques Burnel, the bass player from '70s punk band The Stranglers – he got into him through his dad, who's a big fan. He laughed when I said there's no way my dad and *me* share musical tastes; maybe I'm a bit of a rock chick but I run screaming from the room when Dad sticks on any of his ancient heavy metal albums from the dim, dark past.

"There's a photo of my dad on the bookshelf," I giggle at the thought of it. "It's of him when he was in his own heavy metal band – he's got this terrible beard that's waxed at the very end for some reason, and long hair practically down to his waist!"

"I'd love to see that!" Conor smirks.

We're turning into my street and I can see old Mrs

Harrison at her window. She gives me a wave and a really enthusiastic smile. I've never had a proper conversation with her over the years – just exchanged hellos and waves and comments about rude builders – but she always seems so sweet, so positive.

Maybe that beaming smile of hers is what gives me the confidence to be a bit forward, for the second time today.

"That's my house over there. Do you... um, want to come in for a coffee? I mean, I could show you that photo of my dad, if you'd like."

"Yeah, that'd be great!" Conor replies, straight away, no hesitation.

Despite chattering all the way here, I'm suddenly so stunned and shy that I can't think of one single, solitary word to say.

Luckily, Conor can.

"Hey, listen – I just thought of something..."

Uh-oh. This isn't the get-out clause, is it? This isn't the part when he invents an errand he's got to run for his mum, or paint he's got to watch dry just to backtrack out of my invitation for coffee, is it?

"...my friend Nat's in this skateboarding competition tomorrow afternoon, down at the leisure centre. It could be a laugh. Do you fancy coming with me?"

I think I say yes – I *must* have said yes – because he's smiling and saying "Good". But I've just been zapped into this weird bubble of bliss where I feel totally disconnected from everything around me, including my brain and my senses.

After that, I *must* have opened the front door, because I'm now hovering in the hall, my feet about five centimetres off the floor.

Conor has just asked me out on a date and I am so happy I can hardly wait till later to tell Cherish and Angel—

"Oh…"

I hadn't expected Megan to be home – she's usually still out somewhere with her mate Pamela at this time on a Saturday afternoon.

But there she is, facing me full-on in the kitchen, arms crossed defensively, giving me a ferocious stare like she's daring me to take one more step into the kitchen. I think I remember a documentary recently showing lionesses doing something similar to protect their territory.

Then I'm aware of myself waffling, introducing Conor to my fabulously friendly sister (not) and her shy little friend. I think Megan grunts some form of hello at him, while Pamela does what Pamela does best: giggles and turns prawn-pink.

I hear Conor say a hearty hello, oblivious to the drop in temperature. We've come from the brisk and chilly outdoors into something sub-zero, thanks to Megan's icy glare.

Only right now, it's not as icy as it was only a few short seconds ago; her eyes are flitting between Conor and me and then back at Conor again with an unreadable expression in them. What *is* that look? Is it irritation? Confusion? Curiosity?

Oh, *I* don't know – Megan's too hard to figure out at the best of times. But what I *do* know is there's something about it that's sending a shiver all the way down my spine and straight back up again.

Chapter 3

Witterings and warnings

"I'm sorry, sweetheart, I didn't mean to scare you. I haven't scared you, have I?"

I'd be a lot less scared if Mrs Harrison would stop gripping my arm quite so tightly in her amazingly strong, wiry hand.

"It's just that it's a bit hard to take in," I try to say tactfully.

It's just that this whole thing sounds like a complete load of *rubbish*. Like the deluded rantings of someone going ever so gently but firmly senile.

I mean, none of what this mad old dear has just said can be true, because a) Megan might not be the easiest person to live with, but there's no *way* she "means harm"

– or whatever sinister way Mrs Harrison put it – to me or anyone else; and b) Meg's always been spooked by this woman – she never got over the kind of wariness that all the local kids feel about Mrs Harrison – and therefore she would never, *ever* set foot inside her house for a tarot reading, like Mrs Harrison claimed happened yesterday.

Uh-uh, no *way*...

"I know you're only young—"

Oh, God, please don't patronise me! I think to myself, keeping what I hope is a polite, tolerant smile on my face as Mrs Harrison drivels on. (Mum's always drummed it into me to be nice to the neighbours at all times, but it's proving to be a bit of a struggle right now.)

"—and it's very hard to understand concepts like the spiritual world—"

It's very hard to understand Mrs Harrison, full stop. Urgh... if I'd only been able to find my other glove earlier, if I hadn't faffed about wasting time looking for it, then maybe she wouldn't have spotted me and dragged me into her house. Maybe I'd be well on the way to rehearsal by now, arriving nice and early in the hope of a bit of time alone with Conor. Although there's been so much of that this last week that I can hardly complain. One date at the skateboarding show on Sunday (and several snogs after!) and we were officially going out together. The only time I haven't hung out with him after school this week was Monday, and we met for lunch that day (a baked potato in the precinct and more kisses in lieu of pudding...).

"—and you *have* to believe, dear, that I always, *always* keep my readings confidential," Mrs Harrison trills on, her funny, peachy face powder clogging in the frowns of her forehead. "But this feeling I had about your sister when I was giving her a reading, this malevolence I felt towards you... the message was *so* strong, dear, that I knew I just had to tell you to take care. Do you understand? Does that make sense?"

My blood boils – Megan isn't malevolent; she's just troubled, depressed, severely lacking in self-esteem. Wasn't that the gist of what the doctor told Mum and Dad last year? How dare this woman who doesn't really know anything about Meg, or about us and what we've been through, pass judgement?!

"I'm sorry, but it *doesn't* really make sense," I try to say as kindly as I can, even though I don't feel very kindly towards this woman at all right now. "Meg's fine; she's just a bit introverted, that's all."

"And the scars on her wrists...?"

Oh. So Megan *has* been here? But no – I still don't

believe it. Mrs Harrison must have seen the scars when Meg passed the house one time; when she was in the garden pruning her roses or nosying at neighbours or whatever she does for kicks. Maybe that's it; maybe it's all down to snooping. Mrs Harrison saw the ambulance take Megan away that day last August, and spotted the bandages around her wrists afterwards, even though Meg took to wearing long sleeves from then on. Maybe the old bat put two and two together and got four, even though the rest of our neighbours swallowed the story about Meg having a rumbling appendix.

"It was nothing," I reply defensively, feeling the heat rise in my face. "It was just some dumb thing that she was sorry she'd done straight away. And the scars aren't deep – she didn't really want to... you know, to kill herself or anything."

I feel myself wilt under Mrs Harrison's gaze. It's as if she can see straight into my mind, and knows the part of what I've just said that's true and the part that isn't. It *wasn't* 'nothing'; Mum, Dad and Megan had to go to counselling together and separately for months after it happened. And my sister *wasn't* sorry she'd done it straight away – in fact I don't know if she's sorry about it now, since she's never, ever wanted to talk about it, to me, our parents or the doctors. She likes drawing attention to it though, when she starts with the scratching business, of course...

At least the last bit of what I said to Mrs Harrison is true: the scars aren't deep – no more than bad scratches – so I think (but I guess I don't know for sure) that it wasn't a serious attempt to die (although it didn't seem like that at the time – even just scratches on that part of your body cause pretty scary amounts of blood, as the red-soaked tea towels in our kitchen proved). But if you were going to get all technical and look for evidence to prove that it was more a cry for help than a serious suicide attempt, you could argue the point that Megan chose to use a bog-standard knife-and-fork type knife – though it did have a serrated edge – instead of the butcher's block-worth of scarily sharp carving knives we've got. And, of course, she did it in the kitchen – with Mum and Dad happily (for that moment) watching TV in the living room just across the hall. Within a split second of hearing Megan call out, Mum had beaten Dad through there, with me thundering down the stairs from my room about half a minute later, once the commotion had reached me through the new birthday CD from Cherish that I'd been listening to; Paul Weller's *Days of Speed.*

Talk about a memorable birthday... a straightforward meal out with the family, followed by tense hours hanging around in the Accident and Emergency unit. You know something? I've never been able to listen to *Days of Speed or* anything else by Paul Weller ever since.

Oh God. Do other families out there have to deal with this stuff, this kind of complicated mess? Sometimes it all crowds in on me so much that I can hardly *breathe.* Mum and Dad struggle with it too; it's like this business with Mrs Harrison right now – there's no *way* I'm worrying my folks with her scatty ramblings. Dad only just told me in confidence last night that he's going to get Mum to go to the doctor next week, to get something for her jangled nerves.

"Dear, you're very trusting, aren't you?" says Mrs Harrison suddenly, as she lets go my arm and wraps both her gnarled hands around mine. "But sometimes being too trusting can be bad for you."

The way she's holding on to my hands, the way she's looking at me – somehow they're conspiring to make me cry and I really, *really* don't want to do that in front of her.

"I... I've got to go. I'll be late for this... this thing I'm supposed to be at," I mumble, snatching my hands away and heading for her front door, desperate for the fun and freedom of the band rehearsal and my friends. And my *boy*friend.

"Wait a minute, dear!" Mrs Harrison calls after me, just as I haul her front door open.

I turn to see what she wants, years of inbred politeness overcoming my desire to leave and not look back.

"Did you know that you've got a footprint on the back of that lovely coat of yours?"

The footprint: one dirty great brand of a mark that I spotted on my pale sheepskin coat a week or two ago. Brushing it didn't make it come out and neither did the special stain remover Mum bought. She says she'll drop it in the dry-cleaners sometime next week – see if they have better luck getting rid of it.

"Yes," I say brusquely in reply to Mrs Harrison. "I know it's there."

And yes, I mutter silently to myself, as I close the heavy door behind me, *I know the print looks a pretty good match for the funny treads in Megan's favourite trainers. But I'm trying really, really hard not to think about that.*

Chapter 4

Waiting impatiently

"Oh – Megan's not in here with you, is she, Sarah?" Mum asks optimistically, glancing around my bedroom, as if my sister might be hiding behind the curtains or stashed under the bed or something.

Is Mum kidding? I'm pretty sure the only way Megan would set foot in this room is if she was dragged in – bound and gagged – by a herd of wild horses.

"No – she's in the bath," I reply, hoping Mum can't hear the irritable edge to my voice.

"I thought so, only I just spotted a candle burning in her room when I passed just now..."

Mum won't have liked that; she gets very jumpy about anything that can cause harm (finding a knife that's sharp enough to cut open a bread roll is next to impossible in our house these days). There was a story on the news just last week, I seem to remember, about some family who died after a candle fell over in an empty room; so that'll now be at the top of Mum's list of household terrors, just above leaking gas fumes, electric shocks and accidental drowning.

"I'll just give Megan a knock and check she's OK," Mum smiles a wan smile, as she makes to leave my room. "By the way, are you all right for money tonight? Do you need more for a taxi later?"

"No," I shake my head. "I'll be OK. Conor'll see me home."

And with that, Mum's gone, off to check that Meg hasn't drowned – accidentally or not...

It's just under two weeks to go till the Battle of the Bands competition, as Mr Fisher reminded us at rehearsals today, when Salman kept messing up the intro to the song. (Mr Fisher didn't know what Sal had told the rest of us – that he was at some party last night, and I think beer and too much of it might have had something to do with his lack of concentration.) Anyway, this evening – even before Mum mentioned money for a taxi – I decided that once the competition is past (ie, no more weekend rehearsals), I'm *definitely* going to get a

Saturday job. On our way into town last week, me and Angel saw an ad for Saturday sales girls at that freezer food place on the High Street. Angel nearly died (died *laughing*) when I said I thought I'd maybe phone about it. But then Angel's always stated categorically that the only part time job she'd take is in a clothes shop, ie, a *designer* clothes shop, 'cause then she'd get great discounts. I mean, yeah, if I had a choice, I'd love to work somewhere like that too, but right now I'm more interested in the money and, naff or not, the freezer place has a pretty good hourly rate.

So what's got me thinking about cash all of a sudden? Well, I'm holding the reason for that right now: my acoustic guitar, all polished and immaculate and (most importantly) fixed. It's lovely having it back. Dad picked it up from the music shop for me today. I never thought anything about it apart from how chuffed I was to get my hands on it again: that was until teatime, when Dad made some joke about it costing so much to repair that he might as well have bought me a new one.

Although he was laughing, it made me feel pretty bad – I know things have been kind of tight financially since Mum gave up her job. I think she got that I-should-be-at-home-for-my-kids guilt thing after what happened with Megan. Although I don't think Megan's even noticed

Mum's at home more – she still just disappears into her room and blasts the music up loud as soon as she gets in from school.

She's done that now – blasted the music up loud, I mean. Between that and the Saturday night footie match Dad's roaring along to downstairs, I can hardly hear myself play. And, God... look at the time! I'll have to listen out for the doorbell – Conor should be here any minute.

And instantly, I feel a knot of anger in my stomach. Not towards Conor – no way; it's Megan who's working my nerves. She locked herself in the bathroom half-an-hour ago, after I specifically asked her *really* nicely if she'd give me a knock and let me know before she dived into the bath, so I could get to the bathroom cabinet and stick my lenses in first. And now I'm sitting here on the edge of my bed like a lemon in my ancient, horrible specs, forced to listen to Meg's choice of music blasting from her room while she keeps growling at me whenever I knock on the bathroom door and try and ask her how long she'll be. I'm not vain; really I'm not. I mean, I *know* I don't look like the back of a bus and I'm *truly* grateful for that and would never take it for granted, but when it comes to my sight, well... OK, so there are plenty of nice-looking frames out there, but it's back to the money thing. Mum and Dad have shelled out enough on my contact lenses; I can't go demanding new glasses too.

And if Megan doesn't get out of the bathroom soon, I'm going to have to whip my specs off and just watch the movie with Conor tonight in fuzz-o-vision...

Brilliant. *Now* I feel swamped with guilt for getting annoyed with Meg. So she jumped in the bath and forgot to tell me – so what? I know what this is all about: that stupid conversation I had this afternoon with mad Mrs Harrison. Somehow, she's got me thinking all these insane thoughts about my sister, a whole trail of conspiracy theories I'd never normally give space to in my brain. Like at teatime, I went to put a bag of rubbish out for Mum and spotted my missing black glove at the bottom of the bin. How had it got there? Who knows. Some mistake. It got scooped up with the last bag of rubbish and dumped by accident. I don't know – whatever. But thanks to Mrs Harrison, all of a sudden, I imagined Megan chucking it in there. And it gets worse. I caught myself almost inspecting Meg's trainers tonight, just to see if they *did* match the footprint on the back of my coat. And then the worst of the worst; when I started strumming on my guitar earlier, I suddenly had this terrible suspicion that it *hadn't* broken by accident, that Megan had come up here and deliberately smashed it the night I announced I'd got in the school band.

Isn't that *totally* insane?

A ring at the doorbell – in a nanosecond I place my guitar on the bed and bolt downstairs. I know I saw Conor at rehearsals earlier, but I still get a kick out of seeing him alone, that tummy-fluttering realisation that I actually go *out* with this beautiful boy.

"Hey," he grins as I yank the front door open, "since when did you wear specs?"

Shit! I was in such a rush to answer the door that I forgot to take them off! I feel so exposed: this is like those dreams you get where you turn up to school in your pyjamas, or worse, *naked*.

"I– I normally wear contacts but I just haven't been able to put them in," I bumble, knowing my face is now flushing luminous red. Wow, I must look like *such* a love goddess – *not*.

"They're cute!" Conor smirks at me as he comes inside and scrapes his boots clean on the doormat.

"They're hideous!" I moan, my fingers automatically touching the bulky, black plastic frames.

"Shut up and take a compliment," Conor laughs, then kisses me so that I have to do what he says and shut up...

*　　*　　*

"Satisfied?" Megan barks at me, standing dripping in the doorway of the bathroom, dark tendrils of damp hair snaking limply around her neck and shoulders.

No wonder she's shivering; she's got the tiniest towel in the cosmiverse draped around her. Why didn't she grab one of the huge, fluffy ones out of the airing cupboard? Or use the new dressing-gown Nana bought her for Christmas? It's as if she's deliberately trying to look pathetic; some sad little urchin thrown out on the street.

Listen to me… that's Mrs Harrison's fault again, putting these nasty, twisted thoughts in my head.

"I'm sorry to keep knocking; I just need to get in for two minutes," I try and smile at Megan. "You could wait and then get right back in the bath. Or get right back in it now, I don't mind – I'm only going to stick my lenses in…"

"Forget it," Megan says miserably. "You've spoiled it."

"I didn't *mean* to spoil it," I reply, aware of the tension creeping into my voice. "If you'd let me know beforehand, like I asked…"

"Oh, sorry – I *forgot*," Meg mutters sarcastically. "Your amazing social life comes first. How *silly* of me to forget."

Uh-oh – when she's in this awkward frame of mind there's no point trying to get round her. This is one of those moods she sometimes gets in where she decides I'm this golden child who goes to non-stop brilliant parties and has an all-round, charmed life. Yeah, *right*. Is *she* the one who's going to be sitting behind a till in Freeze-Eeezy Foods this time next month?!

"Thanks," I reply to her in the same bright, brittle tone that Mum uses when she's trying to pretend that everything's fine.

For some reason, my fingers are shaking too much and I can't get my damn contacts to go in first time, like normal. Sod's law, isn't it? If I wasn't in a rush – if me and Conor hadn't been sitting in my room, doing a mini-rehearsal to pass the time till Megan finally got out of the bathroom – there'd be no problem. But we have exactly fifteen minutes to do the twenty-minute walk to the cinema (bang goes the opening credits), and Fate seems to think that it's a pretty funny joke to turn my fingers into a bunch of wobbly sausages. Oh, great – now my left eye has started streaming from one bodged attempt too many to ram my lens in. And look at that... the right one's coming out in sympathy! I guess it's just as well me and Conor are going to a pitch-black cinema; sitting staring at a girl with bloodshot eyes wouldn't have made a great Saturday night out for him.

OK, *calm*.

Five minutes, six disposable contact lenses and two traumatised eyeballs later, and I guess I'm as ready as I'll ever be.

I try to stick a smile on (so Conor will recognise me and not assume a red-eyed alien has just walked in the room) and go to open the bathroom door. And then I spot it, hanging from the hook on the back of the bathroom door: the fluffy, nearly floor-length, white dressing-gown – Nana's present to Megan. Did Meg forget she'd taken it in here? Or was she just so grumpy with me pleading to be let in that she grabbed the first thing at hand, like that practically non-existent towel, I mean?

Who knows, who cares – me and Conor now have *ten* minutes to do that twenty-minute walk...

"Sorry about that, I couldn't get my lens..."

My words tumble away to nothing as I step back into my room. At least I *think* it's my room. Megan might as well have draped a *face* cloth over her boobs, for all the coverage that minuscule towel is giving her, and the way she's sprawled on the floor in front of Conor – one leg stretched out and the other knee bent – it looks like I've barged in on the set of a *porno* movie, for God's sake!

Chapter 5
The many faces of Megan

"Hey – I heard your little sister gave Conor a real eyeful on Saturday night!" says a voice in my ear. "Any chance of inviting me round next time she's doing her strip show?"

I tuck my folder under my arm and let fly with my elbow without missing a beat. That deft dig in the ribs soon sorts Salman out, and I keep straight on walking, eyes front.

"Oof!" he gasps, though I'm sure he's putting it on. I didn't do it *that* hard. "What was that for?! I didn't mean anything by it, Sarah!"

"Oh yeah? So why did you make it sound like a seedy *Carry On* movie then?" I ask him, not slowing down as I stomp along the corridor towards my drama class. It's still five minutes to go before the end-of-lunchtime bell rings, but Mrs Hennessey asked us all to get there early so we can see the whole of the modern version of *Macbeth* she's got on tape for us.

Sal pants as he tries to keep up with my pace now that I've winded him.

"Look, I'm sorry," he says, sounding properly apologetic now. "Conor just made a bit of a joke about it this morning, when we were talking about what we got up to at the weekend. I told him the high point of Saturday night for me was chucking spaghetti hoops at *Blind Date* on the telly, and he said his Saturday night was a whole lot more surreal, thanks to your sister practically flashing her bits at—"

"Stop right there, unless you want to lose your front teeth!" I tell him, only partially fooling around.

"Aw, come on! It's like I told you! He was just making a joke of it!" Sal protests.

"He *better* have made it sound like a joke!" I mutter, a tumble of emotions suddenly crowding my head. Yeah, me and Conor had joked about Megan's peep-show routine on Saturday night, on the way to the movies ("Honest, Sarah, I didn't know where to look! I spent most of the conversation talking to the top of her head, I was so embarrassed!"), but now... he hadn't been boasting to Sal, had he? And Megan, *yes* I'd been mad at her for wafting around on my bedroom floor like a *Playboy* centrefold (and she *knew* I was mad, from the speed she grabbed her towel and scurried out past me), but however much she pisses me off – there, I've said it – this big sister protective thing I feel for her kicks in. It's like, *I'm* allowed to feel frustrated or irritated by the way she is and the things she does, but no one *else* better try that stuff in my hearing. For God's sake, I've never even moaned about her to Angel and Cherish, no matter how unbearable it's been at home, and they're my best friends.

And right now, well, Salman's a laugh, but I've heard the way he talks about girls sometimes and he's not going to get away with being disrespectful about my sister like that. I was even relieved on Saturday when I put it to Conor that Megan maybe had a bit of a crush on him, and he tried to stick up for her: "She's only young, remember, Sarah. She's probably a lot more embarrassed about it now than we are. And she's all right, really; she's a sweet kid."

A sweet kid: I've never heard anyone describe Megan as that before. It's certainly not what my gran would have called her. Unlike Nana, she never minced her words when it came to Meg. "You should watch that one," I heard her tell Mum in the kitchen one day, when Megan had had a strop about me getting nicer school shoes or something. "She's a selfish little madam and no mistake." Mum had gone crazy at Gran for that; it really made them fall out. I think Mum's always regretted that they never were properly close afterwards, specially since Gran died a couple of years ago.

Salman now sprints ahead of me along the bustling corridor, then turns and jogs backwards, a huge, cheeky grin on his face. "Aw, Sarah – don't go all huffy on me for saying something stupid!" he begs me, holding his hands up in prayer position.

I don't tell him he's just about to slam into a whole posse of Year 7 girls and can't hide a smile of satisfaction as he bashes into them, sending them flying like tenpins and tripping over his own feet as he tries to keep his balance.

"Let me carry your books for you at least, just to make up for being a tactless dork!" he jokes, collapsing on to his knees in front of me as the Year 7s dust themselves down and throw him filthy looks (though secretly, I think they kind of *enjoyed* being slammed into by such a hunky sixth-former).

I stop dead, about to snap out some funny line back, when my eyes are drawn to the left, to the rows of industrial grey lockers. At the end of the nearest aisle to me I see a hunched, crying figure. I can only see a pair of shaking shoulders and a face lost in a pile of tissues, but I know straight away that it's Megan's buddy Pamela.

"Catch you later, Sal..." I mumble, leaving him crouched down and confused, with a corridor of giggling girls and sniggering boys now wondering what he's up to.

And Pamela; well she could be doing an impression of me after the drama with my lenses on Saturday night, her eyes are so red and puffy.

"Pamela? What's up?" I ask gingerly. Has something happened to Megan? Those two are always together...

"I hate her. And she's *not* staying at my house next weekend, I can tell you *that* for nothing."

Uh-oh. Dad and me just spent the whole day yesterday persuading Mum to take up Auntie Kelly's invitation for my parents to go and stay with them next weekend (I think Auntie Kelly is as aware as me and Dad that Mum's in dire need of a break). Mum kept protesting that she couldn't leave Megan alone in the house, even with me to look after her, but Dad put paid to that one by phoning Pamela's parents and asking if they'd mind having Megan over to stay. Of course, they were cool about it; Megan and Pamela regularly do sleepovers. Except Pamela is sitting here now, telling me it's not going to happen.

"You can't *hate* Megan! She's your best friend!" I tell her as I lean companionably against the locker next to her.

"Yeah? Well, why'd she chuck a bunch of books at me?"

I'm about to say something joky, when I blink at the sticking plaster on her forehead and the yellowing circle of a bruise that's ringing it.

"It must have been an accident! What happened?"

"We were in the cupboard in Miss Jamal's class, helping tidy it up," Pamela sniffs, rummaging around in her pocket for another tissue.

"Here," I tell her, digging out an opened packet of Handy Andies from my bag. "Go on…"

"Well, she was talking to me about being nearly naked in front of—"

She stops, suddenly realising who she's talking to.

"It's OK. I know what you're trying to say," I shrug.

Pamela doesn't look too convinced, so I give her a little smile of encouragement. Oops – being nice to her makes her instantly turn on the waterworks, but at least she carries on talking.

"I think she thought I wasn't – *hic!* – listening to her or she's jealous 'cause this boy Tariq likes me, and next thing, she's chucked this pile of books down on my head!" Pamela sobs.

I don't want to be this way, but suddenly, I can all too easily picture that dark, angry glower coming into Megan's eyes. It's not too hard to imagine her silently lifting the books and taking aim... God, that's awful of me, isn't it?

"It definitely *had* to be a mistake," I say hurriedly, as much to convince myself as Pamela. "What did you do when it happened? Did Megan take you to the school nurse?"

There's a loud parp as Megan blows her nose.

"No," she continues after a second. "Mr Fisher and Miss Jamal – they came to see what had happened."

"Mr Fisher was there?" I ask, surprised to hear his name in connection with the English department. It's funny, but I guess I feel kind of territorial about him; he's just so funny and nice and human, unlike most of the other teachers at our school. He's the sort of person I think I could easily have a crush on, if he was about ten years younger, of course (ie, before he started losing his hair!).

Pamela doesn't answer my question – she just stares

hard at me as if she's making her mind up whether to say something or not.

"What?" I ask her gently. "Please tell me!"

"Megan tells lies. But it's like she makes herself believe they're true. She does that *all* the time. Did you know that?"

I frown at Pamela. What is she on about?

"She does it *all* the time," Pamela repeats. "Like she copied my geography homework last week, and when Mr Buckthorne accused her of it, she burst into tears. And all the way home, she kept saying it wasn't fair, he was just picking on her and she'd worked so hard. As if I hadn't sat there watching while she wrote down all my answers."

A cold, hard knot tightens in my stomach.

"And last month?" Pamela continues, unstoppable now. "She was moaning about blowing all her allowance on this Wonderbra that she was never going to wear. Well, she didn't blow her allowance on it – I was right beside her when she nicked it out of the shop."

Oh my God...

All those times over the years when things have gone missing and got broken at home; all those times when the finger of suspicion's pointed at Megan and she's cried till her eyes were bloodshot and sworn on her life that she's not guilty. Does this all tie into what Pamela's telling me now?

"And then it's like this thing with Mr Fisher…"

"So what about Mr Fisher?" I ask her in a tense whisper.

"We both heard what he said to Miss Jamal – he was telling her how he needed to get help organising the band rehearsals and stuff," Pamela shrugs.

"And?"

"And then I forgot about it, 'cause we were both in the cupboard talking; me and Megan, I mean," Pamela sniffles. "Then after she threw the books down at me, Mr Fisher and Miss Jamal came running in to see what was wrong."

"*And?*" I say again, desperate for Pamela to get to the point.

"Well, so Mr Fisher was helping Megan tidy the mess in the cupboard, and Miss Jamal made me sit down at a desk just outside, while she went to see if the school nurse was on duty, so she could get her to check me for concussion or something. And that's when I heard what Megan said to Mr Fisher…" Pamela mumbles, her eyes fixed on mine.

"What did she say?" I push her, feeling my heart pound, but not knowing why.

"She told him she was your sister. He sounded all interested, y'know, like 'Wow, Really?' And then she starts saying this other stuff, about how you're always going on at home about how brilliant he is."

Pamela's watery eyes are still locked on to mine, so I know there's more to come than this innocent-sounding piece of information.

"Then Megan started coming out with all this stuff about how your parents are really freaked out – they think there's something not quite right about how friendly Mr Fisher is towards, well, *you*."

I can't respond – I'm too taken aback.

"Mr Fisher starts going on about how that's rubbish and everything's OK, when Megan tells him that your parents are thinking of banning you from the band and everything, 'cause they're worried about him and you. Mr Fisher starts to sound all annoyed, but then Megan says she thinks it'll be all right with your parents if *she's* at rehearsals too, like a secret chaperone."

"What?!" I hear myself whisper, the words choking in my throat.

"I heard him kind of stammering and stuff, and then saying OK, but that's when Miss Jamal came back in the room and got Megan to take me down to the nurse."

I still can't speak – my head is throbbing too hard.

"So Megan ended up sitting and waiting with me in the nurse's office, like she hadn't done anything, like it wasn't her fault I was there in the first place. And she starts telling me this other version of what happened – how Mr Fisher asked her to help him with the band, just like that, out of the blue and everything. She didn't know I'd heard every word. But even if I told her, it wouldn't bother her – she'd just tell me I'd got it wrong. It's just her believing her own lies again, see?"

I nod, not sure I'm capable of much else right now.

"It's not true about you and him, is it?" Pamela asks me bluntly and I wordlessly shake my head.

"I *knew* it wasn't. You go out with that Conor guy and he's really cute. And Mr Fisher's a nice bloke – he wouldn't do stuff like that."

And my mum and dad had never lost one minute's sleep over me and Mr Fisher either, I was damn sure.

"See, *that's* why I hate her. She was my best friend, but she's done lots of horrible things to me and I always let her off. But not *this* time," says Pamela, gently fingering the bump on her forehead. "She's a bitch and she's a bully and she's a *liar*."

The memory comes into my head again, of that conversation I almost stumbled in on in the kitchen, all those years ago, between Mum and Gran: "You've got to watch that one," Gran said.

"Listen, Pamela…" I finally find my voice. "What do you mean exactly? Megan is going to be involved in the *band*?"

I *know* that's what she's saying – I just need to hear it again, to make sure I'm not dreaming. Having a nightmare, more like…

"Uh-huh." She blinks her wet-fringed eyes at me. "I think he got scared: Mr Fisher, I mean."

I stare at her incredulously, practically dizzy with dread.

As Pamela stares back at me, the bell trills violently right above us, and all I can do is mumble "Thanks. You take care," at Pamela before moving off in stunned slow motion towards the drama class.

What was it Conor called Megan that time?

Oh, yeah – *sweet*.

Sweet as a snake and twice as slippery…

Chapter 6
Party hard

I did a bad thing – in a good cause. Does that make it OK, I wonder?

What I *didn't* do was tell my parents what Pamela had said, partly because I don't think they can handle any more bad news right now, and partly because a small part of me doesn't entirely trust what my sister's ex-best mate told me last Monday. I've always found Pamela pretty nice, but she's also a bit dim. Can I really rely on what one girl – who's definitely a couple of sandwiches short of a picnic, bless her – has to tell me? Can the sister who I've known and lived with for the whole of our lives actually be so calculating?

OK, so Pamela was right, inasmuch as Megan has

turned up at rehearsals this week, clipboard in hand at Mr Fisher's right hand, but did it really happen like Pamela said it did? Or was she just mad at the indignity of my sister dropping the books on her head and wanted to get her own back in some strange, twisted way?

Anyway, that brings me back to my bad thing: however much it put Pamela in a bad position, I encouraged Dad to phone up her parents and double-check it was still OK for Megan to stay with them this weekend. I'm sorry if I was helping back Pamela into an uncomfortable corner, but I was thinking purely of Mum. She's been looking so pale and strained this last week, as if all the trauma of the last few months is coming crashing down on her, sinking her spirit. She's got to have a break (I tell you, it was brilliant to see her and Dad set off for the station this morning), and if it meant stepping on Pamela's toes and feelings to make that happen, then that's the way it has to be...

There's another reason I feel bad, of course.

"I've invited Seb, and his mates Bola and John. That's OK, isn't it?" Cherish asks blithely, in our five-minute break before the next run-through this Saturday afternoon.

"Well, no, it's not," I frown at her. "I thought you said there'd only be a few of us? Just us in the band plus a friend each?"

That's the way Cherish sold this have-a-party-while-your-parents-are-away thing. And it's how I sold it to my parents – well, minus the extra friends. And the boys. I suppose I just let them believe that I'd be having a girly night in with Cherish and Angel, and they were more than happy with that. If only they'd known Cherish had plans that even *I* didn't know the full extent of until right this second.

Thank God Megan will be safely out of the house tonight, unable to tell tales. She's over talking to Conor, I see with a shudder, trying to look efficient and important with that stupid clipboard of hers. Mr Fisher, I notice, can't look her in the eye any time she goes near him. Well, I think I know what that's all about…

"Oh, don't be such a bore! Isn't she being a bore, Angel?" Cherish smirks at me, goading me to lighten up.

"Well, as long as it's just Seb and Bola and John," I shrug.

Angel and Cherish give each other a look I don't quite like.

Uh-oh…

There are three things making me feel slightly sick, in the midst of this crammed party, full of people who look like they're planning on having a truly excellent time.

The first thing is these people who are so intent on having a good time – there are loads of them and I have no idea who most of them are. Cherish has told me not to worry, but that's easy for *her* to say, since this isn't her house. Angel hasn't said anything, since a) she's been too busy drinking her own body weight in Bacardi Breezers, and b) she's disappeared somewhere (probably barfing her guts up in the garden judging by the state she was in last time I saw her).

The second thing is Conor. Well, not so much Conor as the way he went funny on me when he saw me talking to Seb earlier. I mean, Seb's in my year; I've known him since primary school and I'm positive – even though he hasn't told me – that he's gay. *Everyone* thinks the same, but they don't say – Seb's a brilliant laugh and is very cool, so what's the big deal? But even if Seb was some ultra-hetero macho man with baby-mothers here, there and everywhere, why should it bother Conor? Can't I talk to another guy without him frowning at me?

And the third thing that's making me feel sick? It's just the tiny, inconsequential fact that my sister has just walked through the door.

"Aren't you supposed to be at Pamela's?" I ask, feeling the blood drain out of my face. What do I say? How do I explain the fifty-something strangers clogging up our house at this precise moment, drinking, dancing and transforming our dull, ordinary living room into a lookalike club night?

"Listen," Megan hisses back at me as she tries to hang her coat up on the crowded rack and dumps her overnight bag on the floor, "I think I live here too or have you conveniently forgotten that?"

"But aren't you supposed to be staying at Pamela's? Isn't that what you promised Mum and Dad?" I repeat, feeling sweat breaking out on my forehead. Christ – what's going to happen? Is she going to tell our parents about this? Give them more grief than they need right now? And why shouldn't she, since it's my own fault for letting Cherish and Angel bully me into this....

"Yeah? Well, I remember *you* promising that you'd look after the house while they're away. So, what if I phone Mum at Auntie Kelly's right now and tell her you've invited most of the school round to ours for a party her and Dad know nothing about?!" Megan snaps at me. "Mind you, I don't even *need* to tell her you're having a party – she'll hear it loud and clear down the phone!"

The feeling that I want to be sick practically overwhelms me. I want to find Conor and bury my face in his chest and hear him tell me it'll be all right. But I don't know how it *can* be all right, and I don't know if I want to bury my head in the chest of someone who gave me a dirty look all because I was talking to an old friend – who just happens to be male.

"How did you find out about the party, Meg?" I ask her in a wobbly voice.

At first, I don't think she's going to answer me, since she's now stomping off up the stairs, her back to me.

"The name's Megan," she snips nastily at me over her shoulder as she continues up the stairs. "I heard about it at rehearsal this afternoon. Conor told me."

Oh…

Was that what they were busy discussing when I looked over at them earlier today? Why had Conor felt the need to tell her? But then I guess it wasn't his fault… he didn't know the hassles and the secrecy behind it all.

"Hey, are you OK, honey-bunny?" a voice calls me from the living room doorway.

And hey, what more proof do you need that Seb is gay? Not only does he wear the best designer clothes I've ever seen, have the sharpest haircut from the trendiest salon in town (they've asked him to be a model for them, in some black and afro hair contest coming up), but he calls me honey-bunny too.

"I've been better. It's just sister stuff," I shrug in reply and go to join him.

He's got a bottle of wine in his hand and pours some into my nearly empty plastic cup.

"God – don't get me started, Sarah. My sisters are great – don't even mind if I borrow their mousse, but my brother... Jesus! I just know he's dying to punch me in the face if I give him one good reason to!"

And Seb is off, telling me tales of life at home and about his borderline homophobic brother and cosseting mum and sisters till I'm practically crying with laughter, even if Seb's situation's got a tinge of tragedy to it. Maybe that's why I have have a soft spot for dark, slightly twisted humour so much; laughing at the bad stuff makes it all so much more bearable.

Then something happens that is totally unbearable.

"Can I have a word with you?"

It's Conor, grabbing me by the elbow and practically transporting me bodily away from Seb, who just shrugs sympathetically in my direction.

"What's wrong?" I frown at Conor, keeping my voice low so that the snogging couples on the stairs don't listen in to our conversation.

"She *said* you'd do this."

"Who said I'd do what?" I frown at Conor again, disorientated after my lovely, feel-good conversation with Seb.

"Megan – she said this afternoon that you love parties, that you're the flirt queen when it comes to them."

How the hell would Megan know what I'm like at parties, flirty (which I'm not) or otherwise? What is she trying to pull here? Apart from my boyfriend, of course.

"You told her about tonight?" I reply, just trying to stick to the facts for now.

"So what? You didn't tell her? I think that's pretty mean, Sarah. She was really upset. Why didn't you want her here?"

I can think of nothing to say. What is there to say? What is there to say that doesn't involve telling Conor everything from A to Z when it comes to Megan, the suicide attempt included? I'm stunned and overwhelmed and don't know where to begin.

And that's when he decides to get mad at me, like I'm hiding something from him or silently admitting to some kind of guilt. I don't know what I expected of this party/not party tonight, but it wasn't that Conor would walk out on me.

She scares me – that's why I'm shaking.

Isn't that pathetic? That your kid sister actually *scares* you? If it wasn't so late, I'd walk over to Mrs

Harrison's and demand she helps me with this one, since she claims to know so much. But it *is* late and I don't have the energy to move away from the kitchen table, never mind leave the house and cross the road to Mrs Harrison's.

Oh, yes, Megan scares me. It's like living with an unexploded bomb crossed with a cobra – there's no telling when or if it's going to go off, or how that poison in its fangs will affect you. Already, I feel drugged and stupid – thanks to a glass and a half of wine and too much shock to take in. How much more am I supposed to deal with? I think the humiliation of running down the road after Conor tonight is tough enough, specially when my heel snapped and I went skidding on the icy pavement, watching, shivering as my knee began to pour blood through the tear in my new cord jeans.

Around me, beside me, wherever, the party continues to spiral to a noisier, wilder conclusion, but I don't even feel part of it as I sit here silently with a bag of frozen peas held to my equally frozen knee.

"What are you doing, Sarah?" Angel giggles, wiggling her way towards me after her long-ago disappearing act.

She walked into the kitchen with Joel, I notice, although he's now standing in the doorway with his mates, looking over in this direction with a smug grin on his face. He's whispering something and his mates all do photocopy-perfect replicas of his grin, slapping their clenched fists against his in some well-done, bro gesture of approval.

Suddenly, I realise all too clearly what Angel's gone and done, and I can't believe she'd be so stupid. Joel is a bit of a looker, no doubt about it, but he's got the worst reputation at our school. And if I'm not wildly wrong here, he's just added my best friend to his list of trophy shags.

"Angel," I hiss at her, pulling her down on to the seat next to me. She thunks down on the chair and gives a drunken giggle.

"You didn't… you didn't just sleep with Joel, did you?"

"Don't remember doing any sleeping!" Angel jokes, widening her eyes at me and holding one finger to her mouth like she's about to say "oops!".

"Angel, for God's sake!" I sigh at the mess she's in, in more ways than one. But I don't see how I can speak practicalities with her when she's this far gone.

"Oh, lighten up, Sarah!" she snaps at me, seeing my disapproving expression through her alcohol fog. "It's no big deal, Miss Prissy!"

And with that she's gone, weaving her wobbly way off somewhere.

Great – my boyfriend and one of my best mates have walked out on me, and my other best friend is too busy playing DJ in the living room to help me get these strangers out of my house.

But every cloud has a silver lining, and mine is the fact that Megan seems to have gone to her room and is staying there. The last thing I need right now is for her to be watching and noting the madness and mayhem going on down here.

Actually, that's what I'd like to do right now – go to my room and shut the door. Only it's my party, isn't it? Even if it doesn't much feel like it.

Chapter 7

The damage done

"Jesus, Sarah! What the hell's been going on here?!"

That's what Dad's going to say the minute he sets eyes on this place. Mum... Mum will probably burst into tears. It doesn't matter that I've been scrubbing and scraping and hoovering and polishing for the last few hours: trying to clean this place up is like trying to mop up a spilt pot of paint with a cotton bud.

I set the alarm for 7am today, even though a) I didn't get rid of the last of my 'guests' till 3.30 this morning and b) I didn't sleep a wink anyway. But I reluctantly dragged myself downstairs, braced myself for a scene of total carnage and I wasn't disappointed. It looked like the place had been burgled, trampled by a herd of rampaging elephants, then used as a squat by every down-and-out junkie and drunk in the neighbourhood. There was mess and trash *everywhere*. It was practically impossible to see the carpet for the empty beer cans and cigarette ends. Some kind of oily, greasy fingermarks were streaked along one wall of the hall. CDs and trampled-on CD covers were strewn all over the living room. The contents of every single kitchen drawer had been pulled out by someone looking *very* hard for something (who knows what). There was sick in the bath, red wine stains on our sand-coloured sofa, broken glasses in the kitchen sink and even a couple snoring in the hall *cupboard*, for God's sake.

Now... well, now most of the surface mess is gone and I've got rid of the couple from the cupboard (never saw them before in my life and I dread to think what they were doing in there before they crashed out). But no matter how much air freshener I spray or how many windows I open, I can't get rid of this cloying fug of booze and fags. I haven't got a clue how to get that red wine stain out of the sofa (Mum will know, but asking her isn't exactly *ideal*), I only just spotted that the birdbath in our tiny front garden has been used as a beer-can bin, I'm completely knackered and I think I'm about to have a panic attack.

Yep... I *am* having a panic attack.

My heart's thundering faster than a drum'n'bass beat and my legs feel like they're going to pack up under me. I use the hoover as support and aim myself at the armchair before I make everything ten times more complicated by passing out. It's bad enough that Mum and Dad are due back any minute now; if they see (and smell) the state of this place *and* spot me zonked out on the floor, it's safe to say Mum is going to assume that all manner of hideous crimes have been committed while I've been home alone (ha!) and that she's a truly terrible mother – when, of course it's more a case of *me* being a truly terrible daughter.

Oh, Jesus...

But it's not just the worry of Mum and Dad's reaction that's twisting my head into stress knots, it's a whole load of other stuff too. Let's see... which of them do I pick first? How about the fact that Megan is spooking me out, coming out of her room today just long enough to grab a sandwich and blank me ominously? What's going on in that unfathomable mind of hers? Is she planning on ratting on me to our parents? But what would be the point in that, since the evidence of me screwing up is everywhere you look? I wish I had the courage to hammer on her door and ask her what she was playing at when she told Conor I was some big flirt, but seeing as I tried to keep the whole party secret from her, I guess I can hardly get on my high horse with her, morally speaking.

Still, that's just *one* of my head-pounding stresses. Another is Conor, or more particularly *why* he hasn't phoned to apologise, or even just to talk over why he flipped last night, after one stupid comment from my sister. I keep checking the phone, in case I missed hearing it ring while I hoovered or ferried the ten thousand rubbish bags out to the bin, but there's been nothing to hear except for a hollow-edged, recorded voice from BT repeatedly telling me "You have no messages". At one point, I checked my e-mails, in case Conor had left me some long, heartfelt ramble, but no.

There *was* one message for me, from Angel, and what she wrote has given me more stress than all the rest of it put together. She's on one massive come-down after the party... I can't imagine the hangover she's got, but raging nausea and headaches probably seem immaterial next to the dread she's woken up with today, knowing that she's just made the biggest mistake *ever*.

'What am I going to do, Sarah? I could be pregnant or anything!'

Oh, Angel... Losing your virginity to a creep who isn't even worthy of kissing the ground you walk on is bad enough. But the fact that you didn't even use contraception...

'I feel like killing myself – I'm not kidding.'

God, what do you say to that? I can't handle this... it's too much like a repeat of what happened with Megan last year, and those sensations are so scary that all I want to do is run away. But I don't – Angel's my friend and I have to help somehow, even if I can't quite figure out the right words to make a difference. I wrote back to her straight after I got her message; some throw-away line about not panicking and another telling her that I'd be in touch later, once I'd faced my parents. And in the mean time, I did what Angel specifically asked me *not* to...

'Please, please, please, I beg you, don't tell anyone else about this – not even Cherish. I couldn't stand the shame.'

But what could I do? I *had* to let her in on Angel's terrible secret – I didn't see that I had a choice, if I was going to be in any way helpful. I just thought Cherish might be more... I don't know... *measured* than me, come up with something that might just make a difference. Her older sister Lilah is cool; I even thought that Cherish might subtly ask her how you go about finding clinics open on a Sunday, so we could pass that info on to Angel.

Not that Cherish has got back to me. Where the hell is she? She wasn't in when I phoned earlier and she hasn't sent a reply to my e-mail either. I feel so, *so* lonely and overwhelmed right now. I wish I had some human contact, someone to talk everything over with and tell me it'll be all right instead of expecting me to just cope, as always. I wish I had the sort of sister I could confide in, instead of one I have to tiptoe around and avoid upsetting. I wish—

"Jesus, Sarah! What the hell's been going on here?!"

"Um, hi, Dad; hi, Mum," I smile wanly at my parents as they stand in the living room doorway and survey the debris...

I hold my breath: those are Mum's footsteps coming up the stairs, and I'm pretty sure I hear the clink of cups and plates. Is she bringing me something? I feel my eyes prickle with tears of relief; there's nothing I'd like more than for her to come tap-tapping on my bedroom door, beaming that sweet smile of hers in my direction and making me feel like all is forgiven.

I hear the tap – but it's not on my door. She's talking to Megan in the boxroom. Meg's in there doing her homework, I guess; I heard the whirr of the printer earlier when I came upstairs. Maybe Mum will come in here next, so I better stop looking so wimpy and wet-eyed and cheer up for her.

And I wait...

...and I wait...

...and I wait...

...until I finally let my expectant smile slip away as I listen to the steady thud-thud of Mum's footsteps retreating downstairs.

What a day. After my birthday ("Unhappy 16th, Sarah!") last year, this must be the second scummiest day of my life.

My heart shattered with every disappointed statement from my parents.

"Sarah, how *could* you?"

"We've *always* trusted you!"

"Where's your sense of responsibility?"

"You of *all* people! I'd never have *dreamt*...!"

"Why did you go behind our backs?"

"Do you have *so* little respect for us?"

"We should have *known* not to go away!"

"You could have put yourself in real danger, with all that drink and drugs around!"

"You're the eldest – what kind of signal does this

send to Megan? Poor Megan... she's only just getting back on track!"

Poor Megan... I didn't bother telling them she hadn't stayed the night at Pamela's – it would just have made things worse. Her turning up at home, mixing with a wild kind of crowd, that would have been my fault too. Yet another black mark on my now totally charred track record. I feebly tried to explain that Cherish and Angel had persuaded me to have more friends around, and that it had all got out of hand, but even as the words were leaving my lips I knew it sounded pathetic, as if I was trying to shove the blame on to someone else.

"Oh, Sarah..." Mum had muttered sadly as she and Dad stared at me with such desolate looks of disappointment that I felt like I'd just broken the news to them that I was a serial killer or something.

After that, the three of us worked silently through the rest of the day, trying to fix up the house to as near normal as it was ever likely to get.

And then I escaped up here, letting another mealtime slip by unnoticed. No one came up to tell me tea was ready, even though the smell of something hot wafted up the stairs an hour or so ago. The phone hasn't rung; neither Conor nor Cherish seem to be in any hurry to contact me. And my own mother can't even bear to bring me a coffee while she takes one to my sister. I feel totally isolated, sucked into some vacuum of misery that I've got no way of climbing out of.

But then, I'm not the only one, I think to myself, feeling a hot rush of adrenaline flooding my veins. *What I'm going through doesn't compare with Angel's problems...*

"Are you going to be on that computer long?" I ask Megan as I hover in the doorway of the boxroom. "There's something I've forgotten to do."

I need to get back in touch with Angel. I still don't have anything constructive to say, no magical suggestions that'll make everything better, but maybe it would just help if she feels I'm out there – in cyberspace at least – for her.

"I'm finished now," says Meg, hurriedly gathering up her pile of papers beside an untouched cup of coffee and plate of biscuits.

I'm not really in the mood to stare at my sister, but even just the quickest glance at her tells me she's feeling guilty; just something about the way she's rushing out of here without a sulk or strop, and the way she won't meet my gaze.

"Thanks," I say as we pass by in the doorway.

Good grief, she even has the decency to pull the door closed behind her. She *must* be feeling guilty...

Settling down in front of the screen, I take a deep breath to clear my head – ready to try and figure out what comforting pearls of wisdom I can chuck Angel's way – when a waft of milk chocolate digestive reminds my stomach of what it's been missing.

The first bite is great; the second bite is better; the third one nearly chokes me... I've just spotted something: my e-mail to Cherish, open on screen behind a bunch of other files. I'd closed it – I *always* close my mail, but Megan can never resist nosing at what I've been sent and what I'm sending. *This* time she hasn't even been clever about it. She hasn't put it away after she devoured this particular piece of gossip. So, *that's* what Meg's guilty look was all about; nothing to do with the bizarre fib she'd told Conor.

Why is she like this, my sister? Why does she keep her own feelings shut up, her own life like a closed book, yet she loves to delve into other people's? She thinks I didn't spot her, but I saw her at rehearsals earlier in the week, nosing through the Filofax Mr Fisher had left lying beside his briefcase.

Still – think positive. At least there's no way she can use what she's read about Angel; there's no way she can twist *that* to her advantage.

Is there?

"You've got to watch that one…" Gran had said.

"I think she means you harm…" Mrs Harrison had said.

"Oh God…" I say, and drop my face in my hands.

Chapter 8
The end of a beautiful friendship... or two

"OK – take a two-minute breather, people, and then we'll run through that again. Uh, Sarah...?"

Mr Fisher walks up to the edge of the stage and beckons me to come closer. I pad over and squat down. Did I muck something up there? That's all I'm good at doing at the moment.

"Listen, I know it's a while off for you," says Mr Fisher, rifling through some papers he's got crammed into a green cardboard folder, "but I thought you might like to look at these..."

"Music colleges...?" I mutter in surprise, balancing my guitar across my knees as I glance at the headed sheets.

I've never mentioned doing music courses to Mr Fisher. Or to my parents. *Or* to myself. Primary teaching... that's more or less what I've fixed my mind on. The teacher-training college in town has a great reputation.

"Don't know if it's something you'd be interested in doing, Sarah, but I think it's worth considering – you've definitely got the talent for it."

I feel myself flushing at the compliment. Behind me, I can hear Sal and Cherish arguing about band names, and I'm glad because that means no one else can hear what's going on. I don't think Mr Fisher's given anyone else in the band this info: I feel privileged and shy and very, *very* flattered.

"But they're all pretty far away," I suddenly frown, skimming through the pages.

"So? What's to keep you hanging around here? The world's your oyster and all that, Sarah!" Mr Fisher grins at me.

What's to keep me? My family, my friends... Well, I don't know about my family at the moment. I think my parents will eventually forgive me for what happened; it might just take a decade or two...

Speak of the devil – a member of my family has just walked into the hall right now, an aura of self-importance around Meg now she's got that stupid clipboard under her arm.

"Um, thanks…" I nod in Mr Fisher's direction, then stand up quickly and walk over to my bag to stuff the brochures inside.

And then I see Angel, coming from the backstage area with a cup of water in her hand. Now's my chance.

"Angel!" I whisper, looking back over my shoulder to check that none of the rest of the band can hear me.

God, I hate all this subterfuge. Cherish has to pretend she knows nothing about Angel's situation, even though we talked about it in depth late on Sunday night, when she finally got back to me. Not that Cherish was much help – all she did was get upset and suggest we pay someone to slash the tyres on Joel's mountain bike, but I didn't see how that was going to solve anything.

And today, Tuesday, was the first time I'd managed to get Angel almost alone – she'd stayed off school yesterday and the only way I knew she was OK (ie, she hadn't chucked herself off the bridge over the bypass) was when I called her house at night and got told by her mum that she had a migraine and was sleeping. Earlier today, I caught a glimpse of her going into her art class – looking pale and gaunt – but never managed to catch up with her between then and the rehearsal after school today.

"Are you all right?" I ask her, aware from her taut, tense face that she's anything but.

"I don't want to talk about it right now," she shakes her head at me and takes a sip of her water.

Great, someone else who doesn't want to speak to me. Conor has done an excellent job of blanking me since the start of rehearsals today. He seemed to prefer to gaze at every square foot of the stage and auditorium than look anywhere in my direction. I feel like a *leper*...

"But, Angel, what's happening with you? Did you go and see the doctor yesterday?" I whisper anxiously, remembering the remark she'd made about the morning-after pill in her e-mail.

"I just don't want to talk about it, OK?!" she replies and I can see she might be about to cry.

It's then that Salman shouts at me to chuck over a new set of sticks to him, and by the time I turn back to Angel, she's gone. We all wait, and wait some more, presuming she's gone to the loo, but time stretches on. Or maybe it just feels that way to me because of this void of silent weirdness between me and Conor.

"Hey, folks – let's just try a run-through without Angel this once, eh?" Mr Fisher suggests, sitting himself down in a row of chairs directly in front of the stage.

I don't know whether he's suggested it to her or not, but I see Megan scuttle off to switch off the main auditorium lights. I suppose it makes sense – this is our last rehearsal before the contest on Friday afternoon and staring out into the darkness does make the whole thing feel more real.

Unfortunately for a dress rehearsal, we are all rubbish.

"He is *so* bugging me," Cherish whispers, casting a dirty look at Sal as we all clatter uncomfortably to a standstill.

Sal obviously feels the same way about Cher, and in five seconds flat they are having a full-scale row about band names that I couldn't be more disinterested in if I tried. Too much else is skewed and bizarre at the moment and I don't care if we end up calling ourselves Hopeless.

I take my guitar off and park myself down on my amp till the fighting blows over. It doesn't. Out in the auditorium, I can just about make out Mr Fisher and Megan talking, and then Meg is off; off to do something very self-important from the way she goes stomping out.

I don't have the energy for any of this. Once upon a time (ie, right up till last week) I couldn't wait for this competition, and now part of me can't wait till it's over, if it means I don't have to have anything to do with Conor ever again.

Oops.

What a liar I am.

All I *really* want is for Conor to tell me this has all been some stupid, tragic mistake and that everything's all right. Then we'll kiss and laugh about it and then kiss some more...

"You complete *cow*, Sarah Collins!" I suddenly hear Angel curse as she comes hurtling through the hall's double doors "You think it's *funny* telling my business to the world? Like my life's some big *joke*?!"

I'm frozen, too paralysed with shock to move. But I've heard her right; it is me that my best friend Angel is yelling at, shooting me looks to kill as she thunders up the short flight of steps flanking the stage.

"Hey, everyone!" Angel bellows at the top of her voice, turning and throwing her arms out wide to an imaginary audience. "I LOST my VIRGINITY on Saturday!! Did everyone in town HEAR that? Or did you all get an E-MAIL about it from Sarah ALREADY?!"

I don't need the ground to open up and swallow me; I need a direct portal to drop me to the Earth's core. This is awful. How did she find out? Has Cherish said something and Angel's taken it the wrong way? But when would that have happened? When I tried to speak to her five minutes ago, Angel had been upset, but not with *me*, I didn't think. Whereas now – now I think I'm in danger of having a mike stand chucked at my head.

Where's Mr Fisher when I need him?

And why is Megan staring up at the stage as if she's enjoying some West End play?

Ah, *wait* a minute...

"You mailed her message to other people? *Not* just me?!" Cherish turns on me next, before I get a chance to mull over my suspicions about Megan.

"No! No, I *didn't*! I only sent it to you, Cher! Honestly!" I shake my head hard.

"It doesn't matter *how* many people you told, Sarah!" Angel starts to sob, sending shivers of guilt through me. "Don't you get it? I asked you, I *begged* you not to tell anyone else!"

"She's right! If she didn't want anyone else to know, then you shouldn't have told me!" Cherish snarls in my direction, before going over and wrapping her arms around Angel.

Excuse me, but has the whole world gone mad and someone's forgotten to tell me? And it's getting crazier. Salman has just come out from behind his drum kit and walked round to stand supportively close to Angel and Cherish, which would be pretty funny – if this situation wasn't so horrible – considering Sal and Cherish were bickering like crazy up till about thirty seconds ago. Conor... he's taken a few steps closer to Angel and co; he's obviously trying to let me know where his loyalties lie, without the dirty job of having to talk to me.

"I was only trying to help, Angel!" I hear the words tumble from my mouth. "I didn't know what to say to you! I thought Cherish might..."

And then I stop when I see four pairs of accusing eyes staring at me like I'm scum. There's no point in this, no point at all... I let the guitar go without a second thought and hear it let out an unhappy groan of notes as it hits the floor.

"Fine. Believe what you want to believe," I mutter in a shaky voice. "I quit."

"Oh, *great*!" I can hear Mr Fisher's voice boom from somewhere up in the balcony as I push my way through the black-out curtains at the side of the stage. "And what are we supposed to do *now*?"

I hate walking out on Mr Fisher – he's probably the only person I know who doesn't dislike me or isn't disappointed in me in some way. Then again, now that I've messed up his pet project, I'm probably not his number one favourite person either.

Well, I think, wiping the tears from eyes as I hurry towards the exit, *welcome to the club, Mr Fisher. The 'I Hate Sarah Collins' club – it's got a growing membership...*

Chapter 9

Too much, too little, too late...

"I have to say I'm very disappointed in you, Sarah."

Tell me something I don't know.

"I really thought you, out of everyone, would be more professional," Mr Fisher shakes his head and stares hard at me.

It's funny, isn't it? Not so long ago I felt terrible for Mr Fisher; I was mortified that he'd been emotionally blackmailed by my lying little sister. And even though he didn't know anything about that – the helpless sympathy I felt for him (just like I was helplessly sorry for myself) – I can't help resenting the fact that he's angry with me now. I just can't take the way his eyes are boring more guilt into my head. There's enough guilt and confusion and unhappiness stuffed in here to last me until I'm an old lady; I don't need another load of it from my so-called favourite teacher. I turn my head and gaze out of the window, only semi-aware of the ice-tipped grass of the school lawn directly outside.

"Are you sure you won't reconsider? It's not too late…"

Friday morning at break, just twenty minutes before the minibus takes Mr Fisher and the rest of the band off to the Forestdean Arena to rehearse for the Battle of the Bands competition this afternoon.

I can't help a wry smile.

"I don't think the others would be exactly thrilled to see me climb in the front seat with you," I tell him, and then immediately see I've made a mistake – he thinks I'm making light of it all; being petty and flippant, instead of stating a truth. The whole week, my former best friends Angel and Cherish have blanked me entirely (it's as if it's easier to hate me than hate Joel, who's the actual *cause* of Angel's misery). And Sal and Conor? Thankfully, I haven't bumped into them once, for which I count my blessings. (Not that it takes too long, since I haven't got many of *them* at the moment.)

"Please yourself," Mr Fisher shrugs, gazing down at the floor and signalling that this meeting is over.

I bet he regrets sending for me now. I bet he regrets getting me those brochures for music college, since I'm so juvenile and ungrateful in his eyes.

"Good luck this afternoon," I mutter as I make my way out of the classroom.

"Thanks, Sarah," I hear him mumble flatly behind me.

Those music college brochures, they're still at the bottom of my other bag. I'm going to go home at lunchtime and tear them into tiny pieces. And poor Mum and Dad: they forked out so much money to repair my guitar and I'm never going to play it again. What a waste.

"Sarah!" a voice pants along the crowded corridor. "Wait a minute!"

I flip my head around to look for the source of the voice, one that I don't recognise straight away.

"I just wanted to ask you something…" Pamela says to me breathlessly, appearing by my side.

A very cute, shy-looking Asian boy with enormous, doll-like eyes is with her.

"What's up?" I ask.

"Is it true you're not in the school band any more?"

They're both staring at me intently.

"Yes. I mean, *no*, I'm not in the band any more."

"It's got something to do with Megan, hasn't it?" asks Pamela bluntly.

"Why do you say that?" I frown at her.

"She likes to spoil things. She tried to break up me and Tariq," she babbles, pointing her thumb in the direction of the boy. "She said she'd gone to ask him out for me, but she didn't – she told him I didn't like him any more. We only found out yesterday, when Tariq's best mate told me what had happened, didn't we?"

Tariq nods enthusiastically. "She's just, like, really jealous or something."

"Or a lying bitch," Pamela corrects him.

Not so long ago, I'd have snapped at Pamela for saying that, but not any more.

"Yeah, but just because she tried to split up you and... and..."

What weird sense of loyalty was making me automatically stick up for my sister, when I knew I was wasting my time?

"Tariq," says Tariq helpfully.

"—thanks. Just 'cause she tried to split you two up doesn't mean she had anything to do with me quitting the band," I say warily to Pamela, although I know deep down that somehow it does. It's just that gullible old me hasn't figured it out yet.

"But she fancies Conor! She told me weeks ago, when you were first going out with him. If she can try and come between me and Tariq, then she could try and split you and Conor up too. And when I heard you'd left the band, I thought she must have said or done something, so you guys wouldn't be together so much."

"Well, she made sure of *that* all right," I mumble in shock. "I'm sorry, Pamela – I've got to go, I'm in a hurry..."

A hurry to get out of here before I'm sick.

"Nice to meet you!" Tariq's voice calls self-consciously after me.

He seems a nice lad – I hope he's a better friend to Pamela than my sister's ever been.

And with that thought in my mind, just as the end-of-break bell shrills, I push the side door open and run straight out of school.

"All right, love?"

It's Mrs Harrison, popping out from behind a withered, leafless rose bush with a set of pruning shears in her hand.

"No," I answer her honestly.

"Here," she says, quickly stuffing her shears in her pocket and holding her hands out towards me. At first, I don't understand what she means and then I realise she wants me to give her *my* hands.

I don't know why, but I do as I'm told.

She turns them palm up, so that the backs are resting on the bristling hedge that borders her garden.

"It'll be all right in time, sweetheart. But it *will* take some time… then you'll know real freedom. In the mean time, you've got to start looking out for number one. Do you hear me?"

I do, but I don't know that I understand. Still, with the jumble my head's in, that isn't exactly a surprise.

"I don't mean that you should be selfish," Mrs Harrison continues, her peach face powder looking an even odder shade now she's out in daylight. "After all, there's plenty of people good at *that* without a speck of conscience to bother them – but that's not you, dear. It's not often I'll say this to someone, but you've got to stop always trying to please everyone else and start pleasing yourself. It's the only way you'll get the happiness you deserve…"

I don't know why, but suddenly I want to cry. And suddenly the one person I really want to talk to is my mum. I know it's been hard, that she hasn't had much time for me 'cause she's been so wound up and worried about Megan since last summer (or make that since Megan's been *born*), but right now I don't feel too self-sufficient. Right now I need her to feel sorry for me and tell me she'll make everything all right.

"Thank you – but I've got to go," I whisper and turn on my heel and run down our street.

I can see the living room light's on – it's a cold, overcast day and the sky's colour is more like a wintry four o'clock than the mid-morning brightness it should be. But at least the light being on means Mum's home, thank goodness.

"Hello? Sweetpea?! What are you doing home, what's wrong?" she panics as soon as she sees me hurry through the front door.

How lovely! How I've missed being called that stupid nickname this last week. I'm Sweetpea again, not the prodigal daughter. With one simple use of my goofy nickname, it feels like the slate is wiped clean. All is forgiven and I could kiss her.

And then Mum spoils it.

"Is it Megan? Is there something wrong with Megan? It's Megan, isn't it? Tell me!"

And then I know I'm wasting my time. Whatever accusation I throw my sister's way, however I try and explain what she's said and done against me, Mum will *always* take her side. She'll bat back everything I tell her with a get-out clause to excuse my sister's every fault: "You must have taken it the wrong way, Sarah"; "Megan's been through a lot, remember"; "I know she can be difficult, but you've got to make allowances for her"; "You know what the doctor said – she's still quite fragile, she needs our support and understanding"; "My God, how can you say things like that, Sarah? Don't you remember your sister nearly *died*?"

Oh, yes, I remember the night it looked like my sister might die. Die of jealousy, because for once, Mum and Dad gave me the full glare of their attention. For one night only, they stopped their habit of always trying to include a reluctant Megan in their every conversation. "Well, sixteen is a very special age, so let's *make* it special, eh, Sarah?" Dad had smiled when he pushed open the door to the poshest restaurant I'd ever been to. Not too posh to make me a birthday cake though, and I practically started blubbing when the lights went down and the entire place sang 'Happy Birthday' to me as the waiter weaved towards me with a cake twinkling with candles. Of course, the only one *not* singing was Megan, who grunted about going to the loo the second my surprise appeared out of the kitchen doorway.

One night.

One *measly* night.

Megan couldn't even let me have that one single, solitary night of feeling special. She *had* to hijack my birthday and turn it into her own drama once we got home.

Thanks, little sis – thanks very much.

"Mum, Megan's fine. There's nothing wrong!" I assure my frantic mother, feeling irritated instead of sorry for her for the first time ever. Maybe if Mum hadn't been such a walkover for Megan all these years, we wouldn't be in the mess we're all in now. Maybe if she'd listened to Gran's advice all those years ago…

"Then why are you home at this time, Sarah?"

"It's the Battle of the Bands today, remember? The whole school got off early so they can go and support them if they want."

Well, *that* lie tripped easily out of my mouth. Whatever next?

"You know, I still don't understand why you dropped out of the band," she frowns at me. "It seems very silly."

Silly, that's me – silly for ever thinking I could count on any support around this place, when all the support Mum and Dad can muster has already been assigned to Megan.

"Like I told you, it was a case of musical differences," I shrug, letting another little lie float into the air. "Anyway, I've got some homework. I'm going to use the time to catch up. 'Scuse me."

"Well, even though you're not involved any more, I hope you still wished Meggie good luck for this afternoon!" Mum's voice drifts up the stairs after me.

"Mum, she's not *in* the band," I reply through gritted teeth, without looking back down at her.

I just want to get to my room and get on with tearing those music college brochures into tiny pieces (and the rest of my room too, the mood I'm in), but before I reach the door, something stops me in my tracks. Megan's door is slightly ajar... and it looks like she's got something new on her dresser. I squint; it's a whole *heap* of new somethings, where normally an old lamp and a pile of her favourite books sit.

I can't resist peeking, seeing what's sparking Megan's interest at the moment, apart from trying to wreck my life, that is.

I don't know what I was expecting, but it certainly isn't this mini-shrine, with a semi-circle of tea-light candles set around a brooding picture of a girl (isn't that PJ Harvey?) and a bundle of what – lavender? – tied with twine next to them. There's a partially burnt piece of paper here too, with snatches of writing still visible.

'He will be mine, he will be mine, he will be mine...'

And what's this?

"*Witch Way Now? – Spells To Make Your Life Special!...*" I read out loud, lifting the book that's lying open beside all this paraphernalia.

It's one of those books that everyone went crazy over

last year – strict parents and moral guardians were up in arms, moaning on about the dangers of encouraging kids to mess with witchcraft, while the teen mags wrote about what harmless fun they were; how they were mostly filled with confidence-boosting advice disguised as something more exotic.

A spell? So is this what Meg's been up to? I flip the book around in my hand and read the heading: 'The It Should Have Been Me! Love Spell'. What's this in aid of? Is she hoping Conor's going to fall for her today? Has she been praying to the dark powers of PJ Harvey that Conor will pull the clipboard out of her hands and kiss her madly?!

"Good luck..." I mumble sarcastically, chucking the book back down on the table and hurrying away from Meg's room, and away from this creepy little hocus-pocus set-up.

But, God, I wish I knew a spell that would stop my heart tearing open every time I let a thought of that boy into my head.

Chapter 10
Shadows and light

"Here… you want this? It's got vodka in it!" the boy asks, sidling up to me as I sit on a bench high up at the back of the darkened seating area of the arena. He's holding out a white plastic cup.

Good grief, I've just been hit on by a twelve-year-old boy. He's from that hip-hop band; the ones who should have won the competition. They were miles better than the goth band and… and whatever it was that my ex-fellow band members had finally decided to call themselves.

"No thanks," I shake my head at the cup, and turn my gaze away from him and back to everyone dancing down below. I hope he gets the message and leaves me alone.

Yeah, *right.*

"I don't remember seeing you around. Were you in one of the bands?" Hip-hop boy quizzes me.

"No, I just came to watch."

And torture myself.

"Well, you missed the coach back to your school then," he informs me of something I already know. "Everyone else left ages ago."

I don't say anything, I'm too busy musing about what Megan's up to. I watched her walk away from the rest of the band a few minutes ago and perch herself on the lip of Stage 2. She's doing a lot of hair flicking and gazing around soulfully, like she's waiting for someone to notice her. Then he did – Conor and her have been whispering together, heads practically touching, for the last few minutes. What could they be talking about it? Meg's starring role, stepping into my shoes?

"Sure I can't tempt you?" asks Hip-Hop boy, wafting the drink under my nose.

The old me would have been nice to him, indulged him. He'd have mistaken my friendliness for interest and I'd have been stuck with him for an hour while he tried to get me drunk and score points with his twelve-year-old mates for snogging an older girl. But it's like Mrs Harrison said, I've got to think of myself more.

"Sorry," I shrug and stand up now that I've seen enough. *More* than enough. "Got to go – got stuff to do."

"What, stuff that's more interesting than hanging out with me?" Hip-hop boy grins cheekily. He's got some nerve, I'll give him that. He should try working that charm on girls his own age; he'd blow them away.

I give him a little wave and a smile for his trouble and veer along the aisle towards the stairs. Actually, I spun that boy a line there. The only 'stuff' I've got to do is get myself out of here without being spotted by anyone I know.

Of course, that wasn't my initial plan, oh no. I didn't mean to sneak in here and play spy unnoticed. The reason I changed my mind and came along here to the Battle of the Bands competition was because I *wanted* to see Angel and Cherish, and even Conor, if I could face it. I know how that sounds – like I'm a glutton for punishment, but honest, it's not that way at all. After I'd tried to talk to Mum earlier, after I'd seen all that surreal, spook stuff in Megan's room, after I'd spread out all the music college brochures on my bed and stared at them, deciding which one to tear up first, it suddenly sank in – what Mrs Harrison had been saying to me, I mean.

So I decided to get along here this afternoon, not to watch the band do their thing without me, but to catch my friends afterwards and confront them. Instead of cowering away in confusion – being sweet, non-confrontational Sarah as usual – I decided I wanted to have it out with them: ask Angel why she prefers to be mad at me instead of Joël; ask Cherish if our friendship means so little that she feels she can flip out at me without giving me the chance to defend myself; ask Conor why he chooses to listen and believe Megan over me. So what if I didn't much like their answers, I just needed to know, for *me*.

Well, that was the plan, till all my new-found confidence seeped away the second I saw Megan – glammed up and smirking – step up to the mike between my not-so-best-friends...

I sat rigid and stunned after that, even once all the rest of the audience had cheered or booed the winners, depending on their allegiance, and filed their way out. I didn't go and find the others, didn't have it out with them, didn't make it up with anyone like I'd half-hoped. Instead, I'd just sat and sat, watching my sister ingratiate herself with my old crowd, until she'd pulled her little-girl-lost routine and lured Conor to her.

The exit door's in sight now, a beam of neon light shining harshly in the corridor beyond, guiding me out of this dark and suddenly claustrophobic hall. I'm almost there; just need to squeeze my way past these girls here... and the DJ decks that have been set up there, and...

Oh.

He must have been asking the DJ for a request. Now he's turning away, en route back to *her*, but he stops dead when he sees me, looking about as glad to set eyes on me as he would be if I was Jack the Ripper and Cruella De Vil rolled into one. Why do I get the feeling that I'm the bad guy here?

"Hello, Conor," I say as boldly as I can.

I haven't done anything wrong, just remember that...

"Hello, Sarah," he replies dryly.

Piss off, Sarah, is what I think he really means.

"The band sounded good," I tell him, hoping I sound gracious and grown-up.

"Yeah, Megan did really well," he says pointedly. "Everyone thought so."

Tell him about all her lies, a defensive voice whispers in my head. *Tell him about her deliberately wrecking your stuff; tell him what she's done to her own best friend; tell him what you've just realised – that Megan's not sad and troubled, that she's selfish and manipulative; tell him that the whole of your childhood – your life – has been messed up by this miserable shadow of gloom that Megan casts over your whole family...*

But as I stare into his hooded eyes, I know that it would be like trying to tell Mum what was going on and expecting to be believed. Just like our parents, Megan's got Conor – and my friends too, by the look of it – wrapped around her little finger. Maybe she's got a real talent for it, this ability to reel people in, or maybe she's just a bit of a witch after all, in more ways than one.

"See you, Sarah," he mutters flatly and moves off.

"See you..." I mutter after him, feeling that familiar and unwelcome tear at my heart.

With a shudder, I pull my coat close around me and hurry out of the gloom of the hall and into the retina-frazzling brightness of the corridor.

Don't look back, don't look back, don't look back, I tell myself, sure that the sight of Megan and Conor together will hurt more than I can stand.

"Sarah?"

A familiar, friendly voice.

I turn quickly to locate it, like I'm searching for a life-raft to save myself sinking into a tide of misery.

"Are you OK?" asks Mr Fisher, taking hold of my elbow just before my shaking legs give way.

"Yeah... I just felt a bit dizzy all of a sudden," I lie,

letting Mr Fisher lead me over to a couple of plastic chairs in the corridor.

"Do you want me to get one of the St John Ambulance people to take a look at you?" he asks, his face full of concern as he sits down next to me.

"No!" I shake my head, desperate to avoid any fuss. "I just realised I haven't eaten today – stupid me! It's probably just that..."

Mr Fisher stares hard at me as if he's not sure if he entirely believes what I'm telling him.

"Listen, Sarah," he says after a couple of seconds' silence, "I'm glad you're here – I just wanted to say sorry for coming down so hard on you this morning. I've just... well, I've just had a bit of extra pressure going on at the moment, but I was wrong to take it out on you."

Extra pressure? Could he be talking about Megan's not-so-subtle attempts at blackmail, just to get involved with the band?

"And I really rate you, Sarah – your talent I mean," Mr Fisher clarified hurriedly, "so I guess I was disappointed that you weren't going to be performing today."

I think Mr Fisher is expecting some kind of response, but something has just occurred to me: it's only been a couple of hours since my music teacher lost his temper with me, but here he is now, apologising and obviously giving me the chance to say my piece, if I want to. Conor, who was supposed to be my boyfriend, has never done that, never once in the last week let me explain or heard my side of the story, whether it was the business of my so-called 'flirting' with Seb at the party or the stuff about me supposedly betraying Angel's confidence. How much could I have meant to him if it's so easy for him to believe the worst of me? And how can I care about someone who doesn't care about me? And, of course, the same goes for Cherish and Angel. Oh yes, if there's one thing I've learned lately – after years of trying to look out for Megan – it's that it's a total waste of your love and your life to care for people who throw it all back in your face.

All of a sudden – at that realisation – I feel a warm wave of relief slip over me. It's like all the unhappiness and disappointment I've been feeling, along with Conor's hold over my heart, is all ebbing away.

"Anyway, I just found out something pretty exciting," I hear Mr Fisher say. "At least I hope *you'll* think it's exciting, Sarah."

"Oh, yes? What is it?" I ask him, managing my first smile in days.

"The organisers of the Battle of the Bands – they've just told me they're organising another competition next term, for solo performers this time. But it's going to be much higher profile, with regional winners going to a schools final in London at the end of the year. They're talking about some great prizes – even bursaries for music schools. I really think you should go for it, Sarah. You're one of the most naturally talented students I've ever taught."

Mr Fisher's words hang tantalisingly in the air and I feel goosebumps prickle over every particle of my skin.

"Hey, you still look a little white," he frowns, mistaking my stunned silence for a sign of illness. "There's a café upstairs – why don't we go up there and get you some water and something to eat? And we can chat more about this competition…"

"OK," I nod, letting him help me to my feet.

We can chat about the competition for sure, and maybe we should chat about something else too: the fact that he doesn't have to worry about what my parents think of him and me, considering that any weird 'him and me' concerns on their part were only ever a figment of my sister's vivid and vindictive imagination. After all, maybe I've always protected her in the past, but I don't owe Megan any loyalty any more; she's made sure of that. The only person I need to be loyal to is myself – isn't that more or less what Mrs Harrison advised me?

"Feeling all right?" Mr Fisher checks with me as we begin to walk towards the stairwell leading up to the café,

I *am* all right, *more* than all right now that Mr Fisher's helped me glimpse a future that doesn't involve being emotionally manipulated by my little sister, or let down by people I thought I could count on (Conor, Angel, Cherish... I'm talking about you). But strangely, I can't help myself; I can't resist turning quickly for one last look back into the hall... and see them straight away – Megan and Conor – slow-dancing to some fast song I vaguely recognise and don't much like.

Maybe it's one of those psychic, sisterly things, but Megan chooses that second to glance over Conor's shoulder, and instantly her eyes smile at me, and the fingers of one hand raise off his neck just long enough to give me a small, victorious wave...

If she's hoping that upsets me, then she's wrong – I watch her and feel nothing but a wonderful, soul-preserving numbness. Once upon a time – up till a few minutes ago, in fact – everything in my world, in my life, was affected by Megan and her moods, but I'm not going to let that happen any more. I've got better things to do; starting now, I'm going to look forward to my bright, shiny future, maybe one that involves a music college in a couple of years time. Yep, I like the sound of that – a .

college far, far away from here, from my past and from Megan. (Better dig those brochures out of the bin when I get home.)

It's not going to be easy, and it's not going to come quick enough, but I'll get there.

Wish me luck. Better still, wish me patience – I think I'm going to need it...

THE KILLER'S COUSIN

NANCY WERLIN

"Tell me," Lily said, as if casually. "How did it feel when she went down?" All the air left the room. Lily was leaning forward, her gaze avid, sucking at mine. "Did you feel... powerful? Even for a minute?"

Recently acquitted of murder, David has moved to Massachusetts to stay with his aunt and uncle and complete his senior year of high school. But his aunt makes it clear that he is not welcome in their house, and his young cousin Lily is viciously hostile. As Lily's behaviour becomes increasingly threatening, David wonders what secrets lurk within her. And the more he thinks about Lily, the more he is forced to deal with the horrors of the past.

Winner of the Edgar Allan Poe Award, *The Killer's Cousin* chills and thrills on every page.

HarperCollins *Children's Books*

Ted van Lieshout

brothers

Can you still be a brother when your brother is dead? Luke often wonders. His brother Marius has died, leaving Luke alone with their parents. When their mother decides to burn Marius's belongings in a ceremonial bonfire, Luke saves his brother's diary and makes it his own by writing in it. And so begins a dialogue between the brothers, the dead and the living, from which truths emerge, truths of life and death and love.

Acclaim from the International Press:
"Van Lieshout has written, in clear and simple language, one of the most beautiful books for adolescents I have read in ages."

HarperCollins *Children's Books*

PATRICIA

cut

McCORMICK

Most of the girls are anorexic. They're called guests with food issues. Some are druggies. They're called guests with substance abuse issues. The rest, like me, are assorted psychos. We're called guests with behavioural issues. And the place is a residential treatment facility. It is not called a loony bin.

Callie isn't speaking to anybody. Instead she watches and listens, absorbing and analysing everything that goes on at 'Sick Minds', the place where she was sent because she cuts herself. Yet Callie finds herself drawn into the lives of the other guests. And discovers she has power over life and death...

"I read *Cut* in one breathless sitting... You will not soon forget a girl named Callie and this remarkable novel."
Robert Cormier

HarperCollins *Children's Books*

DISCONNECTED

SHERRY**ASHWORTH**

"It's hard to know where to begin. I'm not even sure who I want to talk to. Or what I want to say. But maybe if I try to put all the different parts together it will make some sort of sense. So here's my story, and it's for each of you to whom I owe an explanation. But remember, I'm not sorry."

Catherine Margaret Holmes
Loving and dutiful daughter.

Cathy Holmes
A-level, A-grade student.

Cath Holmes
Friend and confidante.

Cat
Risk taker, thrill seeker, rebel.

Will that do as an introduction?

"It's not often that a book makes me think I must go out and find some more of this author's work now, but that's the effect *Disconnected* had on me. I was well and truly blown away."
Fiona McKinlay, teenage reviewer for whsonline.co.uk

HarperCollins *Children's Books*

Mark Swallow

I hereby dedicate my Business Studies GCSE to my father. I don't need it because, Dad, I am the business.

Jack is fed up with other people's decisions. Can't he run his life on his own terms? He's pretty famous at school – Jack Curling, entrepreneur and wheeler-dealer. Still his dad can't see that he's OK doing it his way. So it's time to prove a point. The exam is waiting. Can Jack score precisely zero per cent?

"A sassy book with some strong language and a lot of verve."
The Observer

HarperCollins *Children's Books*

Breakers

Julia Clarke

Bianca is dressed in white, like a delicate oriental bird that has landed here by accident. Before she speaks she lights a cigarette. She only smokes when she's upset. "We're going to have a complete break from London. We're leaving."

Cat no longer recognises her life. Uprooted from the city by their actress mother, she and her younger sister Ana must adapt to living by the sea in Yorkshire. Nothing is the same – it's hard to tell friends from enemies, and truth from lies. Soon Cat finds herself caught up in conflicts as powerful as the breakers pounding the shore...

"Unsentimental, gritty and funny, there's only one possible result: Teenagers 1, Parents 0."
achuka.co.uk

HarperCollins *Children's Books*

ALCHEMY

MARGARET MAHY

*"I am Quando the Magician!" the man cries.
"I work enchantments. But never forget – it
is your job to work out just where the trick
leaves off and the true magic begins."*

Roland has everything a young man
could wish for – good looks, enough
money, a ready wit, sexy girlfriend and a
perfect school record. So the fact that he
committed a petty crime is something he
can hardly explain to himself, let alone
anyone else. Worse still, Mr Hudson, his
teacher, knows all about it, and uses this
knowledge to blackmail Roland into
befriending misfit Jess Ferret. But when
Jess doesn't repond to Roland's confident
advances, he becomes intrigued with the
girl for his own reasons...

Self-empowerment meets the super-
natural in this astonishing new novel from
an internationally acclaimed, multiple
award-winning novelist.

HarperCollins *Children's Books*

IN THE MIDDLE OF THE NIGHT

Robert Cormier

Do not pick up the phone. Let your mother or me answer it. If it's for you, I will hand it over. Alone in the house, you do not answer.

The phone calls come every year, waking Denny up in the middle of the night. Every year, Denny's father calmly answers. He never speaks. He simply listens. But this year it's different. It's twenty-five years since the fire, the terrible tragedy for which Denny's father bears the blame. The tragedy which triggered these calls, year in, year out. This year, Denny has had enough. This year, he will pick up the phone – and face the consequences.

Shortlisted for the Carnegie Medal.

"One of the most tautly written and frightening of Robert Cormier's always scary novels."
Independent

HarperCollins *Children's Books*